A LOVE UNEXPECTED

Jo Ann Brown

Annie's®

AnniesFiction.com

A Love Unexpected
Copyright © 2017 Annie's.

Library of Congress-in-Publication Data
A Love Unexpected/ by Jo Ann Brown
p. cm.
I. Title
                        2017942599

AnniesFiction.com
(800) 282-6643
Hearts of Amish Country™
Series Creator: Shari Lohner
Series Editor: Janice Tate

10 11 12 13 14 | Printed in China | 9 8 7 6 5 4 3 2 1

I *thought this day couldn't get worse . . . I was wrong.*

Sarah Beth King glowered at the horse pulling her buggy along the winding road in the southern half of Lancaster County, Pennsylvania. She wasn't upset with Cinnamon, her spirited bay. She was annoyed with herself for believing that today would be a memorable day.

How many times had she heard someone say half-jokingly to be careful what you prayed for because God heard every prayer and answered it?

"Though not always in the way we expect," she murmured to herself as she guided the buggy across the covered bridge over the stream that bisected the small town of Hickory Meadows.

She didn't worry about anyone overhearing her talking to herself because the noise of the metal wheels and the iron horseshoes on the wide boards echoed like hammer blows into the rafters overhead. As the buggy emerged into the afternoon sunshine, she reminded herself—yet again—that she should be relieved her youngest siblings were happy. The twelve-year-old twins, Lovina and Luann, were well loved by their *Aenti* Neva and *Onkel* Bert, who'd taken them in after *Grossmammi* Miriam died almost two years ago.

Everyone in the family had been worried that taking care of four younger siblings would be too much for Sarah Beth. Her protests that she'd been running the household and the family's farm on her own for the two years since their Grossmammi's first stroke were ignored. Her protests that *she* had promised Grossmammi Miriam she'd take care of the family were brushed aside with assertions that the separation would be only temporary. So the family had been decimated as they'd been twelve years before, when Sarah Beth had been the twins' age, after their parents were killed in an accident while harvesting their cornfields. The twins went to live with Neva and Bert, and Sarah Beth was left to look after her other sister and only brother.

Now Sarah Beth saw the twins no more than once every week or so. Today had been her day to visit them, a trip that took her over an hour each way by buggy. Within minutes of her arrival, her sisters were talking about people she'd never met, events she'd never attended, and plans she wasn't part of. Her beloved little sisters were growing away from her and their older siblings.

That had to change. She'd spoken with her Onkel and Aenti about bringing the twins home, but they reminded her how tough it already was for her to provide for Cora, Toby, and herself.

"How can you expect to feed and clothe two more now?" Onkel Bert asked her.

"Toby is fourteen and finishing up eighth grade," she replied, "so he'll be done attending our school in two weeks. Then he can take over the farm chores, and I can concentrate on earning enough to provide for all of us."

She shared her plans for replacing the family's farm stand and opening a shop next to the house to cater to the busloads of tourists who crisscrossed Lancaster County throughout the summer, searching for "authentic Amish" handicrafts. Her cousins didn't believe she could support a family by selling vegetables along with the birdhouses that Toby built and she painted.

She'd seen the disbelieving glances they exchanged when they thought she wasn't looking, but she'd prove them wrong. She was going to make a success of her shop and get her family back together.

When she had to bid her youngest sisters farewell before heading back to Hickory Meadows, her heart had broken all over again. She vowed to herself—and to God—that she'd have her siblings together under one roof before the summer's end. For that, she'd need Cora and Toby's assistance and cooperation.

Cora did the best she could and was a hard worker, but she had Down syndrome, and that limited the tasks she could do unsupervised. That had meant Sarah Beth depended more on her brother.

But how could she expect Toby to help when he hadn't even come home after school?

Again!

Sarah Beth knew where he was. Where he'd been each time he'd snuck away from the farm during the past two weeks, leaving his chores half-done. As she slowed her buggy in front of a barn that was in dire need of paint, she thought of how often she'd heard the name Elias Stutzman from her brother in recent days. She hadn't yet met their new neighbor who lived on the stream's opposite bank, but Toby talked endlessly of the newcomer who had opened a shop to build and repair buggies in the dilapidated barn that had been empty for more than three years.

After drawing Cinnamon to a stop, Sarah Beth stepped out of the buggy. She secured the reins to a hitching post set to one side of the open door and looked around. The only hint that the barn held a buggy shop was a pair of metal-clad wheels leaning against the once-white clapboards.

She started to walk into the barn but halted when a sound she hadn't heard much in the past year reached her ears.

Toby laughing.

Not the polite laugh when one of them tried to ease the evening's painful silence while pretending their family wasn't incomplete. Or the derisive laugh when she or Cora said something he considered ridiculous, something that happened more and more often since he'd become a teenager.

This was a real laugh, bubbling with amusement and indescribable happiness. She couldn't remember the last time he'd sounded so lighthearted and carefree. For a moment, she was tempted to turn on her heel and walk away and let him have this short respite from the sadness hanging over their house like a dark cloud that never drifted away. She was losing her place in the twins' lives; she didn't want to push her often-rebellious teenage brother away too. Every instinct told her to let him be happy while he could.

She turned to leave, blinking away the tears she'd managed to hold back since leaving the twins.

"Can I help you?" The voice from the barn was too deep to belong to Toby.

Looking over her shoulder, Sarah Beth almost choked on the gasp that clogged her throat. The man who stood in the doorway was definitely not her younger brother. He was tall, almost a full head taller than Toby, who now had to look down to meet her gaze. Instead of her brother's dark-blond hair, his was a rich brown, which shone as if the sun were setting beneath the shaggy strands that needed to be trimmed. He had pewter-blue eyes and a sharply sculptured face, a face that suggested his life hadn't been easy. The skin at the corners of his eyes crinkled as he smiled, and he was instantly transformed. The crags became intriguing planes, and his easy grin suggested that he smiled a lot.

On any other day Sarah Beth might have smiled back, but not today. Flirting with a handsome man was the last thing on her mind. If she relinquished even an iota of her hold over her emotions, she feared the tears burning in her eyes would flood down her face. She wasn't going to cry in front of him. Her pain was too private to share with a stranger.

Looking past him, she used her grief and pain like a curtain to hide her true thoughts.

Maybe her defenses weren't as powerful as she'd hoped, though, because the man asked, "Is something wrong?"

"*Ja*," she said, knowing she must not allow this conversation to last a second longer than necessary. She didn't want him to get the idea she was interested in finding someone to walk out with. Being courted was definitely not a priority. Not when her family was separated as it was now.

And there was something else. The cool, assessing look in the man's eyes didn't quite match his expression, an expression that suggested he was eager to help her set everything to rights. It was as if he were wearing different masks until he found one that he guessed those around him could be comfortable with. *Any man who needs to wear a mask is hiding something*, Sarah Beth thought to herself. Curiosity about what he was trying to keep secret teased her, but she pushed it aside. The wisest thing to do was retrieve Toby and leave.

She went into the shop where her younger brother stood. Toby had grown several inches in the past year, and she would need to let down the hems on his black broadfall trousers again because they inched up his well-worn work boots. His suspenders strained to reach up and over the shoulders of his light blue shirt. On a table behind him, she could see his straw hat next to the red plastic cooler he used to carry his lunch to school.

"What are you doing here?" he asked in a tone that had become all too familiar. The sweet brother he used to be had been replaced by an oft-sullen teenager who seemed uncomfortable in his own skin.

"I'm looking for you." Sarah Beth kept her reply calm, refusing to take the bait in his quarrelsome voice. She was uncomfortably aware of the man—*Elias Stutzman?*—standing behind her. It was almost as if she had eyes in the back of her head that could see through her white *Kapp* and the black bonnet she wore over it.

"Well, you've found me, haven't you?" Toby shuffled his feet against the floor as he walked away from her.

"That's no way to speak to your sister." The man spoke without a hint of emotion, but her brother flinched as if he'd shouted at him. "You should ask for her forgiveness."

Toby muttered something that sounded as if it included the words "I'm sorry" somewhere in the middle. Neither he nor the man said anything else.

What should I do now? Toby wasn't going to cooperate with her. That much was clear. She didn't have time to linger at the buggy shop because she had to return home and do her own chores as well as watch while Cora did some of the preparation work for their supper. Her seventeen-year-old sister was a willing helper, but she needed guidance and structure. When Sarah Beth had left the house earlier in the day, Cora was working in her beloved garden. Sarah Beth wanted to return before her sister decided to start supper on her own.

Toby knew that too. She tried to catch his dark brown eyes, but he avoided looking at her. She couldn't wait until he got over his snit. So what could she do?

The hiss of propane lights overhead lit the space that was no bigger than the milking parlor in the Kings' barn where she and Toby milked their small herd of twelve cows twice a day. No stanchions or milk cans were in sight, however. Instead the space was filled with buggy parts and tools. A half-built buggy, its gray compartment empty inside, was visible near the back door that was wide enough to drive through. Something about the place drew her brother like a bee to honey.

Or was it the man who stepped around her so they were facing each other again? Beside him, her gangly brother appeared even younger and more immature. Had her brother come here because he still missed their *Daed* as she did?

"My name's Elias Stutzman," the man said. "I'm new in Hickory Meadows."

"So I've heard."

He looked startled, and she used his momentary distraction to turn her attention back to her brother. Or she tried to. It wasn't as easy to ignore Elias as she'd assumed. Her gaze wanted to drift back toward him, to admire his powerful shoulders and intriguing face.

No, she wasn't going to let herself get distracted by this *gut*-looking man! She must keep her focus—and her eyes—on bringing her youngest sisters home and rebuilding their family. She wasn't going to pay any attention to how her breath seemed to catch over her rapidly beating heart each time she looked at Elias.

"You're Toby's sister?" Elias asked.

Heat climbed her cheeks, and she hoped she wasn't blushing at his gentle reminder that she hadn't introduced herself. "Ja. I'm Sarah Beth King."

"Ah, so *you* are Sarah Beth." A hint of a grin shadowed the corners of his mouth.

She almost asked him what he meant by that comment but bit back her words. She hadn't come to his shop to learn his opinion of her; she was there to convince her brother to remember his obligations at home.

When she said the latter out loud, she was surprised when Elias spoke before Toby could answer. "You didn't finish your chores before you came over here?" His voice was sharp.

Toby had the decency to hang his head, but his stiff shoulders showed it was little more than a pose. "I would've had them done before supper."

"You told me," Elias said in the same barbed tone, "that your sister agreed to you coming over here once your chores were done."

This time Sarah Beth couldn't silence her gasp. If Toby was lying to his new friend, what stories had he spun for her? Even a year ago, she would have protested loudly if someone suggested her brother was dishonest, but all that had changed since Grossmammi Miriam's death. He was turning into someone else. He'd act withdrawn and sullen one minute before becoming overly animated and bouncing off the walls the next. Her best friend told her to ignore Toby's moods, that they were harmless. She'd believed Edith Lehman, who had five brothers and an equal number of sisters. But maybe both she and her friend had been mistaken.

Elias looked from her to her brother before asking, "You did give him permission to come over here, didn't you, Sarah Beth?"

Ignoring how something delightful rippled through her at how his low-pitched voice caressed her name, she shook her head. She wasn't sure she could trust her own voice at that moment.

"A man's word has to be trustworthy," Elias said, his gaze now drilling her brother. "This isn't what I expected of you, Toby."

"Sorry," her brother said, sounding more sincere this time. Raising his head, he gave Sarah Beth a pleading look. "But if I've got my chores done, can I come over here?"

How she wanted to say yes, but if there was to be any chance of reuniting the family again, she needed Toby to do more than he was already—just as she would have to find more hours in the day to fix up the shop and prepare the goods to be sold there.

Somehow.

Once school was out in two weeks, Toby would need to take charge of the farm and manage it without her supervision. That would allow her more time to fix up the outbuilding along their lane and open the shop, which was their best hope of earning enough money to bring the twins home to live with them again.

Her thoughts must have been visible on her face because Toby snarled something under his breath, grabbed his straw hat, and stormed out without another word.

Sarah Beth felt her shoulders sag. That wasn't how she wanted to convince him to come home and help. As she turned to leave, Elias started to follow. She stopped and shook her head. "I don't want you encouraging him to come here."

"I wouldn't encourage him to disobey his sister." He frowned. "You don't look as if you believe me."

"I'm sure your intentions are *gut*, Elias, but I can't afford to chance following the direction in which *gut* intentions can go. Why don't you stay on your side of the stream, and we'll stay on ours?"

It was starting all over again.

Elias stared at his unexpectedly pretty neighbor. The petite blonde was making herself clear. She didn't want anything to do with him.

It was something he should be used to by now. But he wasn't. Fool that he was, he kept hoping for that sense of belonging he craved. The feeling had always eluded him. He was the kid who was always considered a burden. A duty. The one whom everyone believed was behind any act of mischief or destruction because of the gang of boys—both Amish and *Englisch*—he ran around with. Yet even among those outcasts, he'd been an outcast. The district turned its back on him after pranks got out of hand, and not one member of the *Leit*, the district's congregation, believed that he hadn't participated in the misdeed he later found out was the deacon's son's idea. At that point he realized he would never be judged fairly in that district.

He escaped as soon as he was financially able to and moved to Hickory Meadows in the hope of leaving his past behind him. He'd heard the plain folks in the area were welcoming and had a strong sense of community—something he'd been seeking his whole life. He'd never belonged anywhere or to anyone, and he hoped to change that in his new home in southern Lancaster County.

But if the rest of his neighbors were like Sarah Beth King, those hopes would soon be dashed. Just like the congregation he'd once been a part of, she hadn't bothered to get to know him before announcing she didn't want anything more to do with him.

He wasn't a scared *Kind* any longer, the one passed from one distant relative to another after his *Mamm* abandoned him, jumped the fence to an Englisch life, and never returned to see how he fared. Each home he'd been sent to proved to be less welcoming than the one before it, and his prayers that his Mamm, or even his Daed, whom he'd never met, would come and rescue him so he'd have a family again hadn't been answered.

"So," he asked, letting sarcasm seep into his words, "shall we draw a line in the middle of the covered bridge so I won't cross over to your side by mistake?"

Her cornflower-blue eyes widened, and he regretted speaking so sharply. "That's not what I meant," she replied, and he saw the gleam of tears in her eyes. She raised her head as if the motion would keep those jeweled drops from falling. With a quiet dignity she said, "I must ask you for a favor."

"What?" he asked, softening his tone. If he wanted to fit into the Hickory Meadows community, he couldn't alienate his next-door neighbor within minutes of meeting her. He'd had such high hopes that moving to the area had been the right decision after Toby first stopped by with so many questions.

"If my brother comes over again, send him home right away."

"Even if he's finished his chores?"

She laughed without humor. "When are chores ever done on a farm?"

"True, but he seems interested in learning how to repair buggies."

She folded her arms in front of her dark cranberry dress, and he had to struggle not to grin at what he guessed she assumed was a daunting stance, even though the top of her head barely reached his shoulder. "Toby is my only brother, and the family's farm will be his job."

"What if he doesn't want it?"

"Why wouldn't he want it?" Her astonishment was vivid on her face, which was the same heart shape as the white Kapps worn by the women in this district. "It has been in our family for generations, always given to the youngest son."

"Whether he wants it or not."

She started to answer, then faltered. He could see how much she wanted to assure him that she knew her brother better than he did, and, regarding many aspects of the boy's life, he was sure she did. However, from what Toby had told him, Sarah Beth couldn't see how much her brother despised farming. It was supposed to be the goal of every Amish man to work the land, husbanding the *gut* Lord's creation and bringing forth the harvest to feed his family. Some men, like Toby and himself, weren't meant to answer that call. Their interests and talents lay in other directions.

Did Sarah Beth have any idea how skilled her brother already was with the tools Elias used daily to repair and build buggies? What had taken Elias weeks or even months to learn by trial and error, Toby had grasped with astounding ease. Elias would have gladly taken the boy as an apprentice in his shop, but that would mean leaving Sarah Beth without help on the farm. He knew there was another sister, though Toby never mentioned her working in the barn as he and Sarah Beth did.

He started to explain to her how quickly her brother was learning, but she waved aside his words.

"Will you do me this favor or not?" she demanded.

He realized she had no idea what she was asking of him, but he knew exactly why she was asking. Because it was the *family* farm. She had the family he wanted so desperately, and she wanted to protect it. He respected that and could understand with every fiber of his being her firm resolve. Though he couldn't help wondering if he was making a big mistake, he said, "Ja, I will do this favor for you."

Sending Toby home yesterday afternoon had felt wrong to Elias. The boy had come alive, bursting with questions as he worked in the shop. And Elias had discovered how much he enjoyed sharing what he'd learned with the teen. It gave him a taste of being a Daed or an Onkel passing along the knowledge of his craft to the next generation. That satisfied his soul in ways he hadn't imagined existed.

Was that gratification something one experienced in a family? He hoped so, because he might be a real Daed someday. Not soon, though. He needed to get his business established in Hickory Meadows. So far he didn't have many clients, allowing him plenty of time to spend with the boy as he taught Toby to use the specialized tools for working on buggies.

Whatever the feeling was, he didn't want to give it up. Maybe . . .

No, he told himself firmly as he poured himself a second cup of *Kaffi*, watching the sun rise to paint the sky in brilliant shades of red and yellow. It was worthless to keep second-guessing himself. He'd made a promise to Sarah Beth, and he was a man of his word, no matter what others might believe.

Sarah Beth . . .

He thought about how her fiery eyes had snapped at him when she asked him to stop helping Toby avoid his chores on the farm. As much as Toby had talked about his sister, Elias wondered why the boy had never said anything about how lovely she was. He grinned wryly. Toby probably didn't think of his sister as anyone other than the surrogate parent she'd become since the death of their Grossmammi.

Leaning back against the wooden counter in the kitchen, Elias took a sip of his Kaffi. Too bitter. He'd burned it while lost in his musings. He grimaced and poured the rest of the cup down the sink. He hadn't lingered over his scanty breakfast a single time since his arrival in Hickory Meadows, but today, for the first time, he was loath to go out to his shop. Was it because he knew it'd be empty all day except for him?

Elias grabbed his straw hat with its black band and strode out of the house set in the shadow of the barn holding his buggy shop. Feeling sorry for himself had never gotten him anywhere, and it wouldn't now. He hoped Toby didn't show up today, because telling the boy he couldn't hang around wouldn't be easy. He liked the boy and his enthusiasm. Maybe he could convince the kid to give his sister a reason to change her mind. If Toby pitched in more to help with the chores, Sarah Beth might reconsider and let him come back to the buggy shop so Elias could continue teaching him.

In the strengthening light, he noticed grass beginning to grow in the gravel path between the two buildings. He'd have to get it out before it spread. Pulling weeds was an annoying chore because it just had to be repeated all summer.

He laughed. Now he sounded like Toby when he complained about working on the farm.

Elias opened the door to his shop and almost choked on the remnants of his laugh. He looked around the interior in disbelief. Every tool that had been hanging neatly on the wall was now scattered across the floor. The bins that held small parts had been torn open and the contents dumped. It would take hours to sort out the mess and put everything back where it belonged.

Who would have done this? Someone playing a prank on the newcomer? Or just bored kids? He'd seen the results of vandalism before, and it'd looked like this. He'd been *blamed* for such crimes, though he hadn't taken part in them. Quickly he'd learned that, even in a group of plain people who worked not to stand out from one another, there were always those who could get away with mischief and shift the guilt to someone else.

A shudder ran through him as he recalled the last time he'd seen tools strewn around so wildly. His memory was so vivid that the reek of burned hay and wood soaked with water assaulted him as if he now stood near the smoking remains of what had been a barn. His ears rang with the questions that had been aimed at him that day, questions he'd answered numbly while staring at the destruction. Intentional destruction, according to the barn's owner and the fire marshal and the police chief as every eye focused on him.

He swept those memories aside and shook off the pain. He had a big problem right in front of him. He didn't need to compound the mess by heaping mistakes he'd made in the past on top of it.

Who would wreck his shop? Was it random, or was someone determined to send him a message that wasn't "Welcome to Hickory Meadows"?

A charming face popped into his mind, but he disregarded it immediately. Sarah Beth King might be annoyed that he'd given her brother an excuse to avoid farmwork, but he couldn't imagine her tearing apart his shop.

But who . . . ?

He wasn't going to get an answer just standing there. Going to a corner, he picked up the push broom that had been knocked over. It took him several minutes to find the dustpan that had been tossed to the other side of the barn. He used the broom to push the small parts into a pile and the dustpan for a scoop to put them in a plastic pail. Once he had all the pieces off the floor, he'd sort them out. Maybe in the meantime, he'd find some clue to tell him who'd done the damage and why.

"Wow! What happened in here?"

Elias glanced over his shoulder as he shoved a small mountain of screws and bolts onto the dustpan. His eyes narrowed when he saw Toby King walking into the shop.

"Why aren't you in school?" Elias asked.

"On my way there. I thought I'd stop by and apologize for how Sarah Beth acted yesterday."

Elias's brows shot up. "How *she* acted? She had every right to be upset after she came home and found you missing and your chores unfinished."

Toby shrugged with the fake nonchalance that Elias remembered trying to put on when he was the boy's age. It didn't work for Toby . . . just as it hadn't worked for him. He'd never been able to hide how hurt he was when yet another person he'd hoped he could trust turned away.

The boy bent to pick up a hose that connected the air compressor to the power tools Elias used. Rolling it between his hands, he asked, "Do you know who did this?"

"No." Elias took the hose from the boy and set it on a nearby worktable. "Any ideas?"

Toby shook his head, but he couldn't hide his uneasiness as he rocked from one foot to the other.

"Spit it out," Elias said, knowing the teen had something important on his mind.

"We've had trouble at our place too."

Now *that* surprised him. "With vandals?"

Toby nodded. "Sarah Beth and Cora—that's the sister between us—have a farm stand. They sell vegetables from our garden, and Sarah Beth paints little birdhouses to sell to tourists. A couple of weeks ago, the two tables in the stand were turned upside down. Several of her birdhouses had to be redone, and one was broken beyond repair."

"Did she let anyone know?"

"No."

"Why not?"

The boy abruptly looked away, a sure sign he wasn't going to be totally honest. "I don't know how you did things where you came from, but here, in Hickory Meadows, it's not our way to go to the Englisch authorities."

"I wasn't suggesting she should have contacted the police. Did she let the deacon know?"

Toby's nose wrinkled as if he'd just caught a whiff of something that smelled rancid. "Our deacon is ready to retire, and he doesn't like to get involved in anything other than taking a young man's offer of marriage to the girl's family. The ministers do most of his other duties." Again he shrugged. "I wanted to tell someone the last time it happened, but Sarah Beth said no. You've seen how stubborn she is."

"The last time? The farm stand has been vandalized more than once?"

"Twice this month . . . so far."

Elias could sense that the boy wasn't telling him everything. Toby's brown eyes shifted away from his again and again. Was he hiding something about Sarah Beth or about the vandals? Could the boy be involved with a bad bunch as Elias had been to his detriment? Or was Elias reading too much into what might not be more than a teenager's obvious guilt at stopping at the shop when he should be on his way to school?

As if he'd asked the question aloud, the boy said, "I can't be late for school. If you want to know more about our farm stand, go ask Sarah Beth."

"Perhaps I will." Elias frowned as he glanced around the shop. "After I get this cleaned up."

Toby suddenly grinned. "I'll stop by after school and help."

"You heard what your sister said. She needs you at home to help with chores. Don't come over until you've finished those."

"Which means I'll never get to come back and work with you." Toby rolled his eyes.

"Just get your sister's approval before you come back over."

"You don't know Sarah Beth. She'll never say ja."

Elias had to agree that he didn't know his comely neighbor. But that needed to change straightaway if it was possible that the same person or persons who had ransacked the buggy shop had also damaged her farm stand. It was neighborly to keep an eye out for each other, ain't so?

Why are you trying to justify going to see her? You haven't stopped thinking about her since she came over yesterday. That little voice of honesty wasn't going to let him pretend—especially not to himself—that he only wanted to talk to Sarah Beth about the damage done to his shop. It was one reason, but not the most compelling one.

He watched the boy push his scooter along the road until Toby disappeared over a rise. Turning back to the mess behind him, he sighed. It would take him all day to redd up the mess and get his tools and supplies back to where they should be. Though he hated the idea, he needed to put locks on the doors. It would be foolish to give whoever did this another chance to disrupt his work.

If there was a chance Sarah Beth King could help him discover who'd torn apart his shop, then he needed to get her thoughts on the subject. He'd share any clues he found, assuming he discovered anything. He ignored how his heart thumped with anticipation as he thought about talking with his contrary neighbor again. Maybe the old saying was true. It was an ill wind that blew no *Gut*.

Had she been wrong to burst into Elias's buggy shop and make him promise to send Toby home right away if her brother returned there?

That thought had kept Sarah Beth awake most of the night as she'd tossed and turned in the room she shared with her sister. Getting up would have awakened Cora, who was a light sleeper. She hadn't wanted to upset her sister or her brother. For the first time since Grossmammi Miriam's death, Sarah Beth wished she'd moved into the bedroom nobody used now. Or into the twins' empty room, even though that was a constant reminder of how far away her little sisters were.

Exhausted and still wrestling with her decisions, Sarah Beth was glad she'd had plenty of practice making breakfast for her family. She could walk half-asleep through the process and still turn out something reasonably tasty. Or so she hoped. The biscuits, eggs, and bacon she made tasted like sawdust to her, and Toby hadn't said a word to her during the meal. Cora hadn't complained, but then her sweet sister rarely did.

Shortly after Toby left for school, the back door opened, and Sarah Beth glanced up eagerly. She'd never been so pleased to see Edith walk into the simple white kitchen. Edith was her best friend, someone she'd known her whole life, and Sarah Beth was happy to see her ready smile.

"*Gute Mariye*," Edith greeted them before setting her sewing basket on the clean end of the table. She gave first Sarah Beth and then Cora quick hugs.

When Sarah Beth held on to the hug a little longer than usual, Edith's brows rose, though she didn't say anything. Sarah Beth was relieved. Just being with her friend helped banish her fatigue.

Motioning for her friend to sit so they could begin planning their next quilting project, Sarah Beth went to the propane stove to put the kettle on for tea, leaving her sister to ooh and aah over the colorful scraps of fabric in Edith's sewing basket.

Sarah Beth took a steadying breath before walking back to the table, where her sister's wild strands were close to Edith's fiery red hair that was subdued ever so slightly by her white organdy Kapp. Her round cheeks matched her plump form. She was only a hand's breadth taller than Sarah Beth and had an unbridled zest for life, which Sarah Beth really appreciated that morning.

Today they were going to decide on the colors and pattern for their annual quilt. For the past fifteen years, since shortly after they both turned nine years old, they'd made a quilt together each year. One year the finished quilt went into Sarah Beth's dowry chest; the next it was stored away in Edith's. This year's quilt should have been for Sarah Beth, but she intended to give it to her friend the day before her wedding.

People in the community were going to be surprised when they learned that chatty, effervescent Edith was going to be married to tongue-tied Darryl Glick in the fall. Right now, their betrothal was known only to the bride and groom's closest friends who would serve as their *Newehockers* at the wedding. It was a privilege to be one of the wedding attendants. Sarah Beth looked forward to making the light blue dresses and white aprons that both she, as an attendant, and Edith, as the bride, would wear for the ceremony; no plain bride wore a fancy white wedding dress as Englisch women did.

"I was thinking of a Double Wedding Ring pattern," Sarah Beth said as she put three cups on the table. Her sister always enjoyed being a part of their conversations, though Cora despised quilting. Sarah Beth suspected her younger sister would wander out to her flower garden in a short while. That was where Cora was happiest.

"A *double wedding* ring quilt?" Edith grinned. "Are you trying to tell us something, Sarah Beth? Maybe that you're thinking of getting married too?"

"Don't be silly! It's just the name of a pattern." Sarah Beth hoped her laugh sounded more natural to the other two than it did to her. "After all, Amish women don't wear wedding rings like Englischers do."

"Tell me something I don't know. Like who is this mystery man who's got you thinking about weddings?"

"I know." Cora looked up from arranging the scraps by color, her bright blue eyes glittering.

"Do you?" Edith winked at Sarah Beth. "And who is it?"

Cora put her finger to her lips. "No talking about who's walking out together. Sarah Beth says it's a sweet secret to keep."

Wanting to give her sister a hug and vowing to talk to her later to find out whom Cora had decided her older sister was walking out with, Sarah Beth returned to the stove to retrieve the steaming kettle. Cora was seventeen going on eighteen, but her Down syndrome made her act much younger. As Cora was likely to say anything that came into her mind, no matter who was listening, Sarah Beth had suggested some simple rules to follow when talking with others. Her sister had listened closely. Too bad she couldn't say the same about their brother.

"*Gut* tea!" Cora said with a grin as the fresh scent of mint rose from her cup. "Yummy tea."

"From your work in the garden." Sarah Beth filled all the cups, then carried the almost-empty kettle back to the stove. Sitting across from her best friend, she added, "Cora has added several new herbs to her garden this year."

"Delicious, Cora." Edith gave the girl's arm a gentle squeeze. "And *Danki* for separating out the colors. You are always such a big help. If you want to join us . . ."

Cora shook her head vehemently, then laughed along with Sarah Beth. Edith made the same joking offer every year, and each time, Cora reacted as if she'd prefer to stick her bare hand into a beehive rather than help with the sewing. Sarah Beth suspected that her sister was frustrated by not being able to make tiny stitches by hand. When she'd tried to reassure Cora, her sister had pretended not to hear her.

Pride was despised by the Amish, who called it *Hochmut*, but Sarah Beth didn't chide her younger sister. Cora always worked twice as hard as the rest of them to achieve any goal, so Sarah Beth believed that her sister, whom she saw as a special gift from God, deserved to enjoy her accomplishments and ignore those things she would never master.

"Let's go in the front room," Sarah Beth said, gathering up several stacks of scraps. "We can lay out the pieces and see what fabric we need to buy at Yoder's."

Edith gave a rare frown. "The last time I went there, they didn't have much of a selection. And Mahlon was rude to me when I asked if there were more bolts in the back room."

"Really?" That surprised her. One of their ministers owned the small country store, and his son Mahlon, who was a few years older than Sarah Beth and Edith, had worked there since before he could see over the counter. She'd never heard of him or anyone in the family being uncivil to a customer. "He must have been having a bad day."

"He didn't have to try to pass that bad day on to me when I was having a *gut* one."

Smiling, Sarah Beth spread the pieces of cloth she'd carried in across the hardwood floor. She moved the rag rug off to the side before she went back for the rest of the fabric and the basket.

Cora, taking extra care not to spill a single drop, brought her teacup into the front room. She put the cup on a table by the light brown sofa that had seen better days. "Did it!" She clapped her hands in delight.

Sarah Beth gave her a thumbs-up. "Ja, you did."

Kneeling beside her friend as Cora took her favorite storybook from the shelf by the woodstove and sat in the rocking chair, Sarah Beth shifted pieces of fabric into the intersecting circular pattern that would be the heart of the quilt. She and Edith discussed the background color, and she worked to hide her smile. Edith was trying to get her to say which color she wanted, but Sarah Beth had already decided it would be a luxurious white cotton that would make all the scraps look even brighter. Edith was fond of brilliant colors, always wearing royal blue and deep purple, the only two vivid colors that met the approval of their district's *Ordnung*. Those unwritten rules guided their lives, both in their faith and in secular matters.

When Edith asked her opinion about whether they should use denim along with the thinner cottons, Sarah Beth rubbed a piece of worn denim between her fingers to gauge its thickness and flexibility. "I think it'll work," she said as she stretched to place the fabric back among the other pieces. "How much do you have?"

Before her friend could reply, the inner door in the kitchen rattled, a sign that someone had opened the outer door leading into the small mudroom where they left their boots and coats. Their neighbors didn't bother with knocking.

"Do you want me to see who's there?" Cora asked.

Sarah Beth almost nodded, knowing how her sister liked greeting callers. Yet Cora kept glancing at the book on her lap, a sure sign she was engrossed in the story.

"You enjoy your book," Sarah Beth said. "I'll see who's there."

Pushing herself to her feet, she crossed the kitchen and opened the door. Her eyes widened in astonishment when she saw who stood there.

Elias! What's he doing here?

As if she'd asked the question out loud, he said, "We need to talk, Sarah Beth." He looked past her toward the front room, then grasped her right hand.

She couldn't silence her gasp as sensation flitted from his skin to hers. She hadn't guessed his rough skin could be so warm or his touch so tender as he drew her toward the outer door.

"I need to talk to you alone about something I discovered in my shop." His dark brows lowered as he added through clenched teeth. "Right now!"

3

Sarah Beth pulled her hand from Elias's. How bold he was to grab her! Her astonishment at his impertinence sent a shock through her like summer lightning.

She hated that her voice was unsteady. "Okay. Meet me on the back porch. We can talk there."

He nodded to her and Edith as he went to the door. Pausing, he said, "This is important." He left.

Edith had crossed the kitchen and placed a hand on Sarah Beth's arm. At Edith's touch, no bolt shot along her skin. Of course not! Edith wasn't grabbing her as if she were a newborn calf who needed help to get on its feet, so Sarah Beth didn't react with astonishment.

Astonishment. It couldn't have been anything else. After all, she hardly knew the man.

"Be careful." Edith's gaze focused on the door.

Sarah Beth could think of several reasons for Edith's warning, but she wasn't sure which Edith was talking about. "What do you mean?"

"I've heard talk about Elias Stutzman trying to take advantage of women in his old district."

Sarah Beth was astounded again. Elias had argued about the wisdom of letting Toby come to his shop, but he'd been respectful while she was there. Elias was upset about something. That was the explanation for his inappropriate behavior today.

"Who's been saying that?" she asked.

"They were discussing him at Yoder's the last time I was there."

Edith grimaced. "I know the store is the source of many stories that later are proved false. However, you're my best friend, and I felt I should tell you. I don't like to spread stories when they may not be true, but . . ."

"You've done no one any harm." Sarah Beth squeezed her friend's hand and took a deep breath before she went to the door.

When she went outside, Elias was standing on the narrow porch. He looked over the field and the stream that separated her family's farm from his shop. She thought he'd be pacing because he'd seemed intense and impatient inside the house. Yet he stood there calmly.

No, she corrected herself. It was the opposite, because his shoulders were taut as if he carried the whole world on them. The illusion he projected puzzled her. How could he be upset and appear at ease at the same time?

You don't need to know everything about him!

The thought exploding through her head offered *gut* advice. He was her neighbor and a new member of the district. Nothing more. She'd be wise to keep her distance.

"What's so important?" Sarah Beth asked, then regretted her cold tone. She needed to find a happy medium when dealing with Elias. They were going to be neighbors until . . . Before it could form, she halted the thought about having to sell the farm in order to help support her whole family.

One problem at a time.

He turned to her. Though she'd been fooled by his nonchalant posture, she couldn't be by his intense gray eyes. Something had happened. Something bad. Something he felt she had to know because . . .

Before she could figure out why, her sister Cora yelled a greeting and ran toward the porch. A basket of wet laundry lay abandoned on the grass. Her bare feet slapped the ground and Kapp strings bounced on her shoulders. Blonde hair, a shade darker than Sarah Beth's, flew in loosened strands and curved along her full cheeks.

"Gute Mariye. My name is Cora King." She batted the eyelashes on her bright blue eyes at Elias, startling Sarah Beth. Where had Cora learned such flirtations? "I know who you are. Elias Stutzman. Toby's told me about you, but he didn't say that you're handsome, Elias Stutzman."

"Danki," he said, abashed by Cora's outspokenness.

"Cora!" Sarah Beth interjected. "I thought you were inside reading your book."

"I was," Cora said, "but then I saw the laundry needed hanging."

"Elias and I are talking right now, Cora," Sarah Beth said in an attempt to keep her sister from saying something else to embarrass them.

"*Gut!* I'll talk with you." Cora's artless smile widened. "First I've got a question for you, Elias Stutzman. Are you walking out with our Sarah Beth?"

His cheeks grew ruddy. "No, I'm not. We met yesterday." Was he flustered or trying to keep from laughing? His eyes gleamed when he shot a quick glance at Sarah Beth.

She was relieved. As he'd been with her brother, Elias was tolerant of Cora's outbursts. Sarah Beth hoped that was a sign the rumors from Yoder's Store had no basis in truth.

"Do you want to walk out with me?" Cora asked.

Sarah Beth put her hands on her sister's shoulders and turned her toward the door. "Edith is working on a quilt. Why don't you go and help her?"

"I don't like quilting." Cora rolled her eyes, another expression Sarah Beth hadn't guessed her younger sister knew.

"Go and keep Edith company. You can help her finish sorting her material scraps."

Cora pulled a pout that made her look not much older than their twelve-year-old twin sisters.

The sight yanked at Sarah Beth's heart because she missed Lovina and Luann. Each night when the family sat down for supper, the empty chairs accused Sarah Beth for failing to keep the family together in the wake of Grossmammi Miriam's death. Almost two years had passed, and she was no closer to fulfilling her promise to her siblings.

But she was going to make sure they would be together soon. It was a vow she had made to herself and the family. She wasn't going to break it.

However, right now, she needed to put an end to Cora's outrageous comments.

Sarah Beth opened the door, hoping to get her sister to go inside without saying anything else.

"I want to walk out with Elias," Cora protested. "He's handsome."

Hoping her face didn't appear as flushed as it felt, Sarah Beth said, "Walking out is something you do after a singing or other youth event. Not after hanging half the laundry."

Cora nodded. With a smile and a wave to Elias, she went inside.

Sarah Beth closed the door. She wanted to sag against it while she regained her composure. Cora never filtered her thoughts, but in the past the biggest problem had been her sister complaining about food someone had brought to a church Sunday or a fund-raiser.

"I'm sorry," she began as she looked at Elias.

He waved her words aside. "Your sister is enthusiastic. There's nothing wrong with that."

"Enthusiastic? That's a nice way of saying she blurts out exactly what she's thinking."

"If more people did, wouldn't it be a simpler world?"

"You might not say that if you'd handled hurt feelings as I've had to after Cora states what she has on her mind."

His smile fell away. "People shouldn't be quick to judge others who have challenges they can't understand."

Tears flooded her eyes, startling her. It shouldn't be a surprise Elias was insightful. He'd gauged both Toby's desire to get away from his sisters and her need for Toby's help on the farm.

Though Amish considered handicapped *Kinder* a special gift from God, there were those who could never be comfortable around someone who was different. She was relieved her new neighbor wasn't one of those.

"Are you okay?" he asked, his voice as gentle as when he'd spoken to Cora.

"Danki for understanding Cora meant you no harm."

His smile returned, and she blinked, dazzled by its warmth. "I doubt there are many men who wouldn't be flattered by having a pretty young woman flirt with them."

Sarah Beth started to reply, then halted as she was suffused with a feeling she didn't recognize, one created by a sensation she'd never experienced. She was the clearheaded King, the one who solved problems with rationality and caution.

But every instinct teased her to throw caution aside and lose herself in this man's stunning smile and bask in the fact that it was solely for her.

Instantly she looked away. How did she know that enticing smile was only for her? She had to remember what Edith had said. Edith wasn't a gossip, and she wouldn't have repeated anything if she wasn't worried about the Kings getting involved with a man who had a bad reputation. It might be best to have as little to do with him as possible, especially with Toby—and now Cora—wanting to spend more time with him.

Elias watched Sarah Beth's easy smile fade. He recognized that closed-up look on her face. How many times had he seen it in his life? Too many to count. It was an expression people thought protected him from discerning their thoughts.

In truth, he'd seen that expression so often that he recognized what it meant. The person facing him had heard something and changed their opinion of him.

Not for the better.

He let his breath sift through his clenched teeth. Too bad Sarah Beth wasn't as forthright as her sister and willing to tell him what she was thinking. He'd like to know what truths and half-truths—as well as outright lies—had followed him to Hickory Meadows. The truths, which weren't pretty, he'd own up to without hesitation. He always had.

The half-truths and the scurrilous tales were more damaging. He could act as if he were unaware of the lies hovering around him like a swarm of whining mosquitoes, but he couldn't forget—not for a moment—that others believed the false stories.

Pushing those thoughts aside, Elias focused on the reason he'd come to the Kings' farm. He clasped his hands behind him and faced Sarah Beth. With an unemotional and straightforward explanation, he told her about the damage to his buggy shop.

Her eyes widened as he described the mess left by whoever had broken into the building.

"Oh my!" she gasped. "I've got no idea who would do that. Vandalism isn't something we deal with often in Hickory Meadows."

"It might not have been random."

"Oh."

Again he wanted to demand that she say what she was thinking instead of hiding behind a polite expression.

He was glad he hadn't retorted when Sarah Beth continued. "You may be right. We've had a few incidents the past several weeks. The culprits were teenagers—either plain or Englisch—who went beyond their usual mischief."

"What sort of incidents?"

"We've had produce taken from our farm stand. Things like squashes and pumpkins, which can be smashed."

"Toby told me a table was broken earlier this month."

"It was old, and it may have just fallen apart from years outdoors. It wasn't like when tires are slashed on Englisch vehicles or buggies damaged. That sort of thing is much worse."

"Have there been other incidents as serious as breaking into a shop?"

"Few people here lock their buildings, so perpetrators can open the door and walk in."

"You're avoiding my question." Frustration filled his voice.

She raised her hands as if he were a Kind who needed to be calmed. She must have realized what she was doing because she lowered them. "I'm not avoiding anything, Elias. I'm trying to sort out things by talking aloud. It's how I think."

"As I do. I'm sorry."

"You don't have anything to be sorry about. You're upset, and you have every right to be." She gnawed on her bottom lip. "Are you going to call the police?"

"No. I suspect taking things off the wall and tossing them around the shop will be a low priority for the cops." He sighed. "I should head home and get things straightened up."

As he started to walk off the porch, Sarah Beth called, "I'm glad you told me, Elias."

"You are?" He paused with one foot on the lower step. "I was thinking I shouldn't have burdened you with my troubles."

"'Be of good courage, and He shall strengthen your heart, all ye that hope in the Lord.' That's what it says in Psalm 31. My Grossmammi repeated that a lot. She used to add that a burden shared is a burden cut in half." She smiled sadly. "Grossmammi Miriam had a saying and a Bible verse for every occasion."

He nodded, not trusting his voice. She had no idea how comforting her words were and how seldom someone had spoken like this to him. For so long he'd depended only on himself. The idea of sharing troubles and having those troubles lessened was alien to him, though it was a centerpiece of most plain communities.

"I'll do Toby's chores so he can help you before supper," she went on when he stayed silent. "Toby can continue to work at the shop when he has time—*after* his chores are done."

"You're kind."

She was also lovely, he admitted to himself as he stood two steps below her with their eyes almost level. With the sun glinting off the pale gold of her hair and warming her soft skin, she was a delight to look at. He closed his hands by his sides so he couldn't give in to the yearning to brush his fingers against her cheek in a gentle, exploring caress.

"I'm glad to help." Her trite words brought him back to reality. "I'll try to ask some questions without rousing curiosity. Maybe we'll be able to figure out who messed up your shop and why."

"And discover who stole your produce?"

"Ja. We'll cross two creeks with a single jump."

He chuckled, and she grinned.

"I like that saying," he replied. "Another one from your Grossmammi?"

"Something I heard one of my twin sisters say."

Elias stared at her in astonishment. "Twins? You've got other sisters beside Cora?"

"Toby hasn't mentioned Luann and Lovina?"

"No. Are they older or younger?"

"Younger. Twelve years old." Sorrow filled her eyes, surprising him until she added, "They haven't lived with us for nearly two years."

More questions flooded his mind, but he refrained from asking them. He didn't want to upset her further, particularly when she'd offered to help him find whoever had invaded his shop. Like her, he could make a few careful queries and learn more. But his questions would be about the sisters Toby never spoke of.

Once he found out what was happening with the King family, maybe he could find a way to ease the grief that had stolen the glitter from Sarah Beth's eyes. He wanted to bring back their happy glow again. It was the least he could do when she'd offered to help him.

4

Later that week, Elias was beneath a buggy, checking its front axle, when he heard the door to his shop open. Twisting his head, he saw a pair of scuffed work boots.

"Anyone home?" called a voice he recognized.

It belonged to Harry Fitzgerald, his landlord. The Englischer lived about eight miles north of Hickory Meadows near the small town of Strasburg. He owned properties throughout the county, and he'd been glad to rent the barn and house to Elias because they'd been empty for three years.

The week after moving in, Elias had filled his wheelbarrow a dozen times with dirt and debris from both buildings. He'd dumped it into a pile near where a garden once had been planted.

Pushing his way from beneath the buggy, Elias stood and waved to Harry. He motioned for the other man to come over to where he was wiping his hands on an oily cloth.

Harry was a generation older than Elias. His hair was the color of the unpainted concrete floor, and he was thin and very tall. When he walked toward Elias, he resembled a tree waving in the wind.

"Gute Mariye, Harry," Elias said, standing by the side of the buggy that was going to need more repair than its owner, Abe Yoder, the owner of the store in Hickory Meadows, guessed. Once he finished talking with Harry, Elias would have to drive into town and see if Abe wished to have it fixed or invest the money in a new buggy. "What can I do for you?"

His landlord rocked from one foot to the other as if standing on hot coals. The older man's smile appeared strained, and there was a definite quaver in his gruff voice. Harry was nervous. Why? What was going on?

"I came to talk about what I could do for you," Harry said with feigned affability.

"I can't imagine what that could be," Elias replied honestly, hoping that would encourage his landlord to be as frank. "You've been generous, including the big house with the barn."

"The house is big, isn't it?"

"It is." Elias waited, still cleaning his hands with the cloth. Harry hadn't driven to the shop to comment on the obvious.

"Much too big for a bachelor. It'll be expensive to heat when winter comes."

Again, Harry was spouting the obvious. Elias didn't see any reason to explain—as he had when he'd first seen the property—how he planned to use only a small portion of it. He needed a kitchen, a bath, the living room, and a single bedroom. The rest of the house could be winterized and left unheated.

Harry had been the one to talk him into renting the buildings in the first place. Elias had been startled when the Englischer had approached him at Yoder's Store at the Hickory Meadows crossroads and offered to lease him the buildings for a reasonable rent. Several times since, Elias had seen the older man at the store, and they'd chatted, but Harry had never acted so oddly.

So what had changed?

When Elias didn't reply right away, the older man began to shift again uneasily. Something was wrong.

Elias had no idea what. He'd paid his deposit and his rent on time and in cash. He'd fixed the barn and the house, and they were in better condition than when he'd moved in.

So what was Harry's problem?

As if Elias had voiced his thoughts aloud, Harry said, "I'm sure you're curious why I'm here today."

"You could say that."

"I wanted to ask if you'd be willing to move."

Elias tossed the cloth into a bucket by the rear wheel of the buggy. "Why?" He watched Harry's face closely, but he couldn't ascertain anything except that his landlord was nervous. Two drops of sweat appeared between Harry's snowy brows.

"Because I've got another property available that I think will be a better fit for you. It's closer to the village of Strasburg, and you'll get more buggy traffic there than you will here where there aren't as many plain folks. Getting people to know you're around and open is important when you're starting a business. Nothing builds a business faster than word of mouth. Here you don't get a lot of people passing by."

The man kept listing reasons he believed Elias should relocate his business. He barely took a breath. Either Harry had practiced his pitch or he was trying to guarantee he wouldn't be interrupted until he had his say.

"Danki for thinking of me," Elias interjected when the man stopped long enough, "but I'm happy here. I've got as much business as I can handle now."

"The other place is a good site, Elias." Harry began to cite statistics of how many cars would go past each day and how the businesses on either side—two antique stores—were faring.

Elias listened, though nothing Harry said gave him a reason to change his mind. The traffic at antique shops would come from Englisch tourists. For a buggy repair shop, he'd learned that tourists could be a nuisance if they came in while he was trying to work. Each asked similar questions and acted irritated when he didn't stop to answer them. Some tourists seemed to believe that an Amish business was some sort of museum.

Why was Harry pressing him so hard to move his business closer to Strasburg? It couldn't be because of the recent vandalism, could it? Harry hadn't said anything about not wanting to rent to Elias any longer after the damage done to his property. That would have made sense, but he wanted Elias to move from one of his properties to another.

Why?

Harry must have sensed Elias's continued reluctance. "At least look at the other building I've got in mind for you," the older man insisted. "You're a shrewd businessman, and I don't want you to lose out on a great opportunity."

Elias started to say that flattery wouldn't change his mind either and he didn't have the time to waste. He halted himself. Was he hesitant to leave because his business was doing well where it was? Or was there another reason he wanted to stay in Hickory Meadows?

Glancing toward the window, he took in the view of the stream, the covered bridge, and the Kings' farm beyond it. He hadn't spoken with Sarah Beth since he'd told her about the vandalism, but he'd replayed that conversation over and over in his mind. Each time, he was suffused with the same longing to find the culprits so she and her family wouldn't be victims again. She hadn't complained, but he guessed she didn't have a lot of extra money to spend on replacing items for her farm stand.

Take advantage of this offer and leave before you get drawn into her life. Have you forgotten how many other times you've tried to trust someone, and how you've gotten hurt in return every single time?

He listened to the rational side of his brain. The advice was *gut*, based as it was on what had happened in the past.

"All right," Elias said. "I'll check it out."

"I can drive you there now."

He shook his head. "I've got to get started on this buggy today. Why don't I plan on seeing the property in a few days?"

Harry wasn't pleased with his answer. However, the older man nodded and offered to give him a ride to visit the property.

What else could Elias do but agree?

That was one of the many questions he had as he bid Harry a *gut* day. Something wasn't right.

But what?

"What do you think, Edith? Will it work?"

Sarah Beth stood in the middle of the dusty interior of the building that once had been a chicken coop. Years ago someone had banished the chickens to the coop near the dairy barn. She guessed this building had then been used for equipment because one wall had double doors. Each door had a big window in it to match the ones on the opposite wall. Why had someone put windows in an outbuilding door? She had no idea, but the windows and the doors could come in handy.

She watched her best friend turn as Edith took in the raw wood walls and the open rafters above their heads. The floor's planks were even, though there were spaces between them wide enough for Sarah Beth to slip her smallest finger between. A few blades of grass poked through them.

"It'll need a lot of redding up," Edith said, but her eyes were bright with excitement. "It's *gut* that we aren't afraid of hard work. Will you whitewash the walls?"

Nodding, Sarah Beth outlined her ideas for the building she wanted to turn into a shop to replace what remained of the rickety farm stand by the road. There was space next to the building for parking, and its proximity to the house should keep it safe from vandals. The shop would be big enough to allow her to sell her birdhouses and Cora's vegetables. In addition, she hoped Edith would provide quillows to draw in tourists. A quillow was a smaller quilt that when folded within itself could be used as a pillow. The tourists loved them because they were smaller and less expensive than a quilt. Her other neighbors might be interested in selling their wares as well as volunteering to work in the shop. That would allow Sarah Beth to balance the shop with her chores in the house.

It was the way, she was sure, to earn enough money to prove to her Aenti and Onkel it was time for the twins to return home. Two years with the family separated was too long. She'd proved she could provide for Toby and Cora, though the money in the bank was almost gone. With the last of it, she could make a pleasant but simple shop to appeal to tourists looking at Amish farms and covered bridges. A sign by the road would invite passersby to stop and check out what the shop had to offer.

"Count me in," Edith said with a grin. "My sisters will be interested in selling crafts here too."

"Do you think you can convince your Mamm to bake a few pies each week?"

"I'm sure she'd be interested. With so many daughters to plan weddings for, she and Daed are always happy to earn extra money to put aside for the future."

That set Edith off on her own wedding plans. She'd spoken of her plans often in the past month, so when she began listing the foods she wanted to serve on the day she married her Darryl, Sarah Beth listened with half an ear. The main meal at Amish weddings was almost always the same: roasted chicken and stuffing with the fixings, including creamed celery.

They went into the house, and Edith smiled at the collection of birdhouses on the table where Sarah Beth had left them to dry. Most were decorated with patterns for quilt squares. Her favorite one was the Wild Goose Chase. Triangles in red and black and green and blue looked like a flight of geese running across the painted square. She'd done two houses—a tall narrow one and a short square house—in the same colors.

"I didn't know you painted birdhouses with sports themes." Edith bent to examine one house set to the side.

Instead of a quilt square painted on it, Sarah Beth had decorated it on one side with the logo for the New York Giants football team. She'd attached a small pennant with the same logo to one corner of the house.

"I put a football on the other side," Sarah Beth said, picking up the house and turning it so Edith could see the dark brown oval decorated with darker laces. "I thought I'd try something new. What do you think?"

"I like it." Edith chuckled. "The other ones you've painted will appeal to Englisch women. This one would catch an Englisch man's eye." She laughed again. "Or the eye of my brothers. They're such football fans. They grab the newspaper first thing every Monday morning to read all the details on the weekend games."

The short-case clock hanging on the wall in the kitchen chimed four times. Edith grabbed her bag off the chair. She stuffed in the squares she and Sarah Beth had sewn for their annual quilt. They had finished about a third of the ones they'd need for a full-size quilt.

"I didn't realize it was so late," she said. "I promised Mamm I'd be home half an hour ago to help start supper."

Sarah Beth gave her friend a hug and stepped back to let her leave. She needed to get her family's supper started too. There was a leftover macaroni-and-tomato casserole from yesterday's lunch. She'd warm that and serve it with biscuits, because yeast rolls wouldn't be ready by supper.

"Cora!" she called.

Her sister's biscuits were the best Sarah Beth had ever eaten, better even than Grossmammi Miriam's. While Cora mixed a batch, Sarah Beth would make chocolate chip cookies for dessert.

She called to her sister again as she took eggs from the refrigerator. When she got no answer, she set the eggs on the table and turned to check if Cora was lost in a book. Cora had rediscovered Laura Ingalls Wilder's stories and was reading the whole series again from cover to cover.

A splat came from behind Sarah Beth. With a soft groan, she rushed to the table and caught the second egg before it rolled off too. Setting it where it wouldn't move, she got a damp cloth.

Kneeling, she gathered the shards before she scooped up the egg. She tossed both into the bucket where she kept scraps to add to their compost pile. She sopped up the eggy mess with the cloth.

The back door opened. Sarah Beth shifted and gasped. Cora was walking into the room with her hand on Elias's arm.

"See who's here!" Cora exclaimed. "It's Toby's Elias." She grinned at him. "We're walking out together. Or is it walking *in* together when we come into the house?"

Elias gave Cora a quick smile as he edged his arm from under her fingers, but his expression as he turned to Sarah Beth was somber.

"Elias, I didn't expect to see you again so soon," Sarah Beth said.

Instead of answering, he held his hand out to her. She hesitated and glanced at her sister who was smiling at the handsome man whose broad shoulders seemed to fill the whole room. She raised her fingers and placed them on his wide palm. A rush of that incredible sensation surged through her, and she bit her lip to keep a gasp from escaping.

As soon as she stood, she released his hand and turned to put the damp cloth in the sink. She set Cora to work making the biscuits. Only then did she look at Elias.

"I need to talk to you." He motioned with his head toward the living room.

She followed him. "Has there been more damage to your shop?"

"No, but this *is* about my shop."

"I told you. Toby must complete his chores before—"

"You made yourself clear." His expression remained serious, but his eyes sparkled before growing serious again. "This doesn't have anything to do with Toby."

"Then what?"

"Do you know Harry Fitzgerald?"

"I've seen him around Hickory Meadows. Don't you rent your shop from him?"

"I do, but he dropped by today and pretty much demanded that I look at one of his other properties. It's north of here, closer to Strasburg. He says I'd get more traffic there."

She tried to ignore her uneasiness when he spoke of leaving Hickory Meadows. Toby had been a changed boy since he'd begun working at Elias's shop. Her brother now did his chores without complaining.

And . . . She didn't want to think about the "and."

"Strasburg is much closer to the tourist areas," she said, "and you'll get plenty of Englischers coming by."

"Englischers don't own buggies, so they don't need my services. I can't see how moving to Strasburg would help my business, but I told Harry that I'd go and look at the property he has in mind for me."

"So you're actually considering leaving Hickory Meadows?"

Before Elias could answer, she heard her brother cry, "You can't go!" Toby stood in the doorway between the kitchen and living room. His hands were clenched in fists at his sides, and tears glistened in his eyes.

Sarah Beth wanted to embrace him at the sight. Her younger brother tottered on the cusp between being a Kind and becoming a man. She took a single step toward him.

Toby edged away. Or was he moving toward Elias? She realized her brother had forgotten about her as he raised a finger and pointed it at their neighbor.

"You told me you'd teach me everything about fixing buggies." Toby's voice was raw with his unshed tears, each accusing word sounding as if it were scraping his throat. "I agreed to do my chores so I could learn from you. Now you're walking away?"

"I didn't say I was going," Elias replied.

That reasonable tone wasn't going to work on her brother, Sarah Beth wanted to tell him.

She didn't have to because Toby fired back, "You're going to look at that other place. If you like it better, you'll go. You don't care what happens to me, do you?"

When Elias fumbled with an answer, the boy stomped away.

Elias started to follow, but Sarah Beth put out her arm to block his way. He could have pushed her aside. Instead he stopped.

"Talking to him when he's upset," she said quietly, "is a waste of time and breath. He won't listen until he calms down."

"What about you?"

"He won't listen to me either."

Elias shook his head. "That's not what I meant. Will you listen to me?"

"It seems you've said all you have to say, ain't so?"

"I've said I agreed to look at the other property. It would have to be something special for me to move there, but if it's *gut*, I need to consider it."

"You're going away?" cried Cora from the kitchen. "How can you be my boyfriend if you go away?" Her lower lip trembled as her eyes began to fill with tears.

Elias started to apologize, but Sarah Beth said, "I think you should go. It's not going to be easy calming either of them."

He looked from her to Cora and flinched as a door slammed upstairs with Toby's frustration. Muttering that he was sorry, Elias edged around Cora and out the door.

Soothing her sister, Sarah Beth convinced her to finish making the biscuits. Hearing the *clip-clop* of iron horseshoes, she went to the front window and watched Elias's buggy drive away. She hadn't realized he'd driven to the house. Upstairs she heard the heavy sound of Toby's footsteps as he strode from his door to his bedroom window as the buggy turned toward the covered bridge.

Were her brother's thoughts identical to hers? A silly question, when she wasn't sure what she was thinking.

But Elias was starting a business just as she was. She couldn't fault him for wanting to make his business successful. Every entrepreneur, Amish or not, shared the same goal. After all, wasn't that what she was trying to do with having a nice shop on the farm to replace the worn-out farm stand? Make her dreams of having her family together come true?

Was Elias pursuing a dream too? Did his buggy shop mean more to him than merely a source of income?

She had to stay focused on *her* dream: bringing her youngest sisters home. Nothing and nobody—no matter how handsome and how giddy and unsteady he made her feel when he touched her—must get in the way of that dream.

Too many people had come into her life and left, taking a piece of her heart with them. Grossmammi Miriam had died. The twins had been taken away by relatives who tried to assure her and Toby and Cora—unsuccessfully—that it was for the best.

Elias had swept into their lives like a breath of fresh air, delighting Cora and giving Toby something to be excited about while Elias had offered her a way to help her brother discover what he wanted to do once he was finished with school.

Now Elias might be leaving.

Like too many others had.

5

Church was held that Sunday at the Waglers' farm, the farthest home in the district from the Kings' house. Toby drove their family buggy, which gave them room to sit and still have space for the dishes Sarah Beth and Cora had prepared the night before. The food was for the midday meal the Leit would share after the three-hour service was finished. No cooking or any other chores should be done on a Sunday. Only work necessary to take care of their animals was permitted.

Sarah Beth had helped her brother with the milking so they wouldn't be late for church. Toby was too young for youth events in the evening. In a couple of years, Sarah Beth would milk late on Sunday afternoons to allow her brother to attend singings and other gatherings. But tonight he'd return home by himself so Cora could enjoy spending time with the other unmarried young adults.

As she had for the past year, Sarah Beth wished she could leave when Toby did. She was older than the young people who attended singings in order to spend time with someone they wanted to walk out with. She didn't have time for courting. Not until her family was united again.

When she heard Cora talking about "her boyfriend" from the moment Elias arrived to join the other men waiting to go into the Waglers' spacious house for the service, Sarah Beth decided it might be a *gut* idea to attend the singing. Perhaps spending time with other young people would distract Cora from the infatuation that had lasted longer than Sarah Beth had expected. Her sister's previous crushes had come and gone almost in the same breath.

She put those thoughts from her mind as she entered the house with the other unmarried women and took a seat between Edith and Cora on a narrow, backless bench. They faced the men on the other side of the room.

Elias was across from them, and Sarah Beth was relieved when Cora didn't mention that once during the long service. Keeping an eye on her sister gave her the perfect excuse not to look at her handsome neighbor herself.

After the last song had been sung in the slow, unison style of their tradition, Sarah Beth herded Cora ahead of her. They needed to leave so the men could rearrange the benches into tables for the shared meal. The men would be served first, and then the women and Kinder would eat with more leisure.

Because many hands were cooperating, the meal and the redding up afterward went swiftly. The midafternoon sunshine was warm and welcoming when Sarah Beth emerged from the crowded kitchen a couple of hours later.

She scanned the yard to discover where her brother and sister were and what they were doing. The motion had become automatic because, even though her siblings were growing up, they remained her responsibility. Toby and a group of his friends were making a temporary ball field. Cora sat under a tree, busy talking with two young Mamms who were feeding their *Bopplin* while they watched a game of horseshoes.

"They're busy, but what about you?" asked Mahlon Yoder as he stepped from behind another tree, startling her.

Mahlon Yoder resembled his Daed, Abe, who owned Hickory Meadows' general store. Like his Daed, Mahlon was broad-shouldered and stocky. He looked like one of the cardboard boxes stacked at the back of the store for customers' use. He had a wide face and an easy smile. The biggest difference between them was that Mahlon had a full head of blond hair unlike Abe's bald pate.

He gave a rueful laugh. "Sorry for frightening you. I thought you saw me."

"I was lost in thought." She took a steadying breath. "There's no need to apologize."

"Are you staying for the singing tonight, Sarah Beth?" he asked.

"Cora wants me to stay."

"She's not the only one." He gave her a warm smile.

Sarah Beth was too amazed to find a quick response. Why was Mahlon acting—out of the blue—as if he were interested in her? They'd grown up together, attending the same school as well as the same church on Sundays. Until they graduated from the one-room school, he'd made her life miserable almost daily by stealing her lunch or pushing her during recess. He'd seldom done anything cruel when an adult was around, but he had bullied and threatened other scholars who tried to come to her aid. He'd taunted her for being an orphan and had called her beloved Grossmammi names because Grossmammi Miriam had scolded him several times for picking on the smaller Kinder.

Once they were no longer in school, Mahlon ignored her. He avoided waiting on her when she came to his family's store and hadn't attended her Grossmammi's funeral. The latter wasn't astonishing because Sarah Beth had wondered, more than once, if Grossmammi Miriam was the only adult who ever saw through the ready charm he slathered on his elders.

But now Mahlon was smiling at her as if they'd been best friends their whole lives and was hoping they could be more.

She suppressed the shiver of distaste rippling down her spine at the idea of walking out with Mahlon. He might be able to forget their shared past, but she couldn't. She'd always forgiven him, because that was central to her beliefs, yet she wouldn't allow him to treat her as he had before.

Deciding the best answer was an innocuous smile, she gave him one before she strolled away as if she didn't have a care in the world. She risked a glance back and saw him scowling. Had he been sincere? Had she hurt his feelings? That hadn't been her intention. Sparing her own had been.

It was astonishing to think she might owe *him* an apology. She faltered. Letting any hurt fester would be as unkind as he'd ever been.

Cora ran up to her. "Sarah Beth, stop them!"

"What? Stop whom?" She wished her sister would start at the beginning of a conversation rather than in the middle.

"They are flirting with *my* boyfriend." Cora pointed at a group of young women who were encircling Elias as if he were a flower and they were a swarm of bees. She jammed her fists against her hips and pouted. "They shouldn't do that."

"No, they shouldn't." She needed to soothe her sister before Cora said something to embarrass herself in front of the Leit. The congregation treated special members like her sister with kindness and forgiveness, but someone might laugh, and that would devastate Cora.

"Tell them to stop!"

Taking her sister's hands and folding them between hers, Sarah Beth said, "I know you think Elias is handsome."

"He is! My boyfriend is handsome." Cora's voice rose with every word.

Before heads could turn to discover what was upsetting her sister, Sarah Beth said, "A handsome man like Elias is accustomed to being flirted with. You should let him handle it."

"I should?"

Sarah Beth sent up a prayer of gratitude to the *gut* Lord because, for the first time, the fury was dimming in Cora's eyes.

"Ja," Sarah Beth said, releasing her sister's hands and putting her arm around Cora's shoulders. She had to be careful how she spoke to Cora, because her sister was apt to repeat her words at the worst possible time. On the other hand, she needed to keep her sister from getting upset about her one-sided relationship with Elias.

"They shouldn't be flirting with my boyfriend." Cora wouldn't budge on that.

"Remember that among the plain people, we keep to ourselves who we're walking out with. Those girls can't know if or who Elias is courting."

Cora considered that for a moment. "True."

"You need to be careful too."

"Me?" Cora's eyes widened so far that they looked ready to jump out of her head.

"Like Elias, you shouldn't let anyone else know you're walking out with someone." Realizing she might be creating a bigger problem for herself in the future, Sarah Beth hurried to add, "Except your sister, of course. Sisters always tell each other everything about the boys they like."

"I like Elias." There was so much childlike wonder in Cora's voice that Sarah Beth gave her a quick hug.

"The secret has to stay between you and me."

"And Elias?"

She resisted her temptation to laugh at the naïve question, because she was accustomed to Cora changing from adult to Kind and back in the space of a single question. "It would be better not to talk about walking out with him either. Let the boy come to you and ask you. You don't want to be seen as a girl who chases after boys."

Again Cora thought about her words. "That makes sense. Danki, Sarah Beth. You're a *gut* big sister. The best."

"You're my favorite, Cora." She hugged her sister again, longer this time.

Pulling away, Cora waved to a woman who smiled at her. Cora rushed to talk to the woman whose name Sarah Beth couldn't recall. She was visiting from their bishop's other district and was related to the Waglers.

Sarah Beth sighed.

"That sounds either very sad or very happy," said Elias from behind her.

How long had he been there, listening to her conversation with Cora? Not long, she realized, calming herself. Why was she always so emotional when Elias was around?

That was a question she wasn't going to ponder.

"Neither," Sarah Beth replied as she faced him. "It's relief."

"Am I being too nosy if I ask why?"

"Ja." She smiled at his astonishment at her quick answer. "However, I'll tell you because I think you'll be relieved too. I convinced Cora she shouldn't share with anyone—not even the boy she's interested in—that she's interested in him."

Elias grinned. "How?"

She explained.

When he laughed, heads turned. There would be talk about her and Elias, but as she wasn't walking out with him and had no intention of doing so, she'd let the gossips gossip.

"You're a *gut* big sister," he said.

"That's what Cora said."

"Cora is wise in ways others aren't." He grew serious. "She gauges easily what other people are feeling, and she never hesitates to offer kindness when she believes it's needed. She doesn't care if you're young or old. She talks to everyone, but she doesn't spread rumors. She sees the best in everyone." He squared his shoulders and sighed before adding, "That may be her greatest gift."

"I'm glad you see her that way. Too many strangers look at her and think she's incapable of doing anything." She rubbed her hands together as she watched her sister cheering when the crack of a bat announced a home run. "She has the same feelings as any girl her age, but I worry about her walking out with someone. In some ways she's a Kind, and that will never change."

"In other ways she's a woman."

"Therein lies the problem." Sarah Beth sighed. "She knows what she should do and what she shouldn't. I hope . . ." She laughed without much humor. "I sound like every parent since Adam and Eve, worrying about their Kinder and hoping it'll be okay."

"We must trust God as our Father to watch our Kinder and speak in their hearts to guide them."

Amazed, she looked at Elias. "That's what my Grossmammi always said." When she laughed again, it was more genuine. "Are you sure you aren't an old *Grossdawdi* in disguise?"

She put her fingers to her lips, but it was too late. The teasing words had already escaped. Would Elias be insulted by them? Or would he think *she* was trying to flirt with him? She hadn't meant her question to do either.

Her dismay eased when he chuckled before saying, "Though there are days I feel as old as any Grossdawdi after crawling around under a buggy, I can reassure you that I'm not there yet. Sarah Beth, your sister listens to you and what you've tried to teach her. In fact, I suspect she has you to thank for the gains she's made."

"My parents and Grossmammi Miriam . . ."

"They may have been *gut* examples for you, but *you* are the one who has been closest to her while the two of you were growing up. You're the one who, as I've seen, doesn't treat her differently. Cora expects others to see her simply as another pretty young Amish woman."

"That's the problem."

"You'll keep reminding her of what she should and shouldn't do, and she trusts you to tell her the truth about what's best for her. As you have with Toby, and I'm sure you do with your younger sisters. Do you see them often?"

"Not as often as I'd like, and I miss them, Elias." She folded her arms in front of her as if she could suppress the pain burning in her heart. "The last time I visited them, Luann and Lovina were annoyed. They wanted to go somewhere and do something with their friends, and I was in the way."

"You said they are twelve. Weren't you more focused on friends than family at that age?"

She shook her head, blinking back the tears that welled up in her eyes. "My parents had just died, and my sisters and brother looked to me. At least Cora did. The twins were just Bopplin."

"I should have realized that. I'm sorry for saying that, Sarah Beth. Forgive me."

"I would forgive you, but you've got nothing to be sorry for. It was God's will my Daed and Mamm were called home to Him. To rail against His plan for them and for me would be *dumm*. I'm sure you agree."

Elias did agree that being angry with God's plan was a waste of energy. However, he wished he could tell her how blessed she was to have siblings and a family who cared for her. Perhaps her family cared too much because they kept the twins away from Sarah Beth, Toby, and Cora.

Maybe he'd know what to say if he'd ever had a real family himself. When it came to families, he'd been on the outside looking in like a puppy with its nose pressed to the door. He'd wanted to go in and be a part of a family. He might not have been able to wag a tail as a puppy did, but he'd have shown his family how much he appreciated their welcoming him.

He'd never had a chance. It wasn't always his relatives' fault. When he became desperate for someone to notice him, he'd fallen in with the wrong crowd. It'd been led by Roy Swartzentruber, the son of the local deacon, who hadn't believed his beloved son could be involved in mischief. Even when their pranks had led to near disaster and the event that had altered Elias's life as much as his Mamm abandoning him had, Roy had never been accused.

Only Elias, the boy everyone expected would come to no *Gut*, had been blamed.

He wasn't that boy any longer. He was a man who'd found a way to give himself a second chance. He wasn't going to let it slip through his fingers. The best way to ensure that was to act as if his past had never happened.

So he kept Sarah Beth talking, easing her distress until she smiled. He noticed the eyes glancing their way, but he ignored them.

"I'll tell you a secret." He chuckled, determined to keep their conversation inconsequential in case somebody decided to eavesdrop on them. Not lowering his voice, he added, "I'll tell you if you won't share it with everyone. I'm not sure how this would be taken by the bishop."

"What's this secret?"

He enjoyed how her cornflower-blue eyes twinkled in anticipation of what he might say. He would have happily gazed into them for an hour or two, but he realized he needed to give her an answer.

"I've got a Boston Red Sox cap I like to wear when I'm reading the sports news in the paper."

"What an outrageous secret!" She laughed, and he wondered if any bird's song could be as lovely as that trill. "So you're a baseball fan?"

"I've been a fan of the Red Sox since I was a boy." He grinned. "My cousin was a Yankees fan, so I decided to cheer for Boston to annoy him. Somehow, as the years passed, I became a real Red Sox fan."

"Toby follows the Phillies, and if they go into a slump, so does he."

"A true fan."

He was about to say more, but his eyes were caught by another pair of eyes. They weren't like the others who'd looked toward him and Sarah Beth. These narrowed ones were set in a frowning face a few yards away. The man, built like a Kind's toy block, glowered at him and Sarah Beth.

Why? He'd seen the man somewhere before today, but he couldn't say where. It wasn't as if he'd done anything to make the man furious with him, because Elias knew he'd recall that.

Or was the man angry at Sarah Beth? Elias realized the man was scowling at her.

"Who's that guy looking like he bit into a lemon?" he asked.

After she glanced to his left, she arched her pale brows. "That's no way to describe our minister's son."

"But accurate?"

"Definitely." A smile teased her lips. "That's Mahlon Yoder."

"I thought I recognized him. His Daed is Abe Yoder, who owns the store in town, ain't so?"

"Ja. The Yoders have run the store for almost a century." She smiled ruefully. "Ask him. He'll be glad to tell you as he does everyone when he has the chance."

"He's giving us ugly glares. Any idea why?"

She rolled her eyes. "He was flirting with me earlier as if I were the last girl on earth."

"If you want to . . ."

"*He* was flirting with me. Not the other way around."

"You don't like him?"

"He's a member of the Leit, and I respect that."

He accepted her polite words. Her sister spoke her mind without considering the consequences, but Sarah Beth's thoughts came through as clearly. From her pose with her arms folded in front of her and her right foot tapping the ground, it was obvious to him that she found the topic of Mahlon Yoder unpleasant.

That realization shouldn't have pleased him as much as it did. Caring about which guy flirted with Sarah Beth was silly. It *should be* silly, but the truth was he didn't like the idea of her spending time with a man who could stare at her so icily.

As if he'd said something to challenge Mahlon, the minister's son swaggered toward them. "You're Elias Stutzman, ain't so?"

"I am, Mahlon," Elias answered without a hint of emotion as his gaze slid toward Sarah Beth for a second. Dismay had returned to her face. Putting an end to this conversation—even though it'd barely begun—would be the best thing he could do.

"How is your little shop doing?" Mahlon gave him a superior smile. "The last one there failed. Not enough traffic coming by. Guess you didn't consider that when you let Harry Fitzgerald talk you into taking the buildings off his hands."

He could tell Mahlon how mistaken he was, but he didn't feel the need to educate the boorish man.

"It's doing well. Danki for asking." Looking past the man as if he'd vanished, Elias smiled. "Toby's coming up to bat, Sarah Beth."

"Oh, I want to cheer for him!"

"Me too." He spared Mahlon a glance. "Toby King is my new apprentice, so I want to see what else he can do well."

If Mahlon replied while they walked side by side toward the field, Elias didn't hear it. He could feel the man's stare piercing his back, but he paid it no mind.

"Danki," Sarah Beth said as they paused to watch Toby take a swing at the ball and miss.

He nodded, not wanting to say anything to disparage another member of the community. He was tempted to tell her that he'd be glad to come to her rescue anytime. Again he remained silent. He hoped she wouldn't have to deal with such rudeness again. He'd enjoyed getting her away from the sour man.

He'd enjoyed it far more than he should have. He needed to be careful, but getting more involved with Sarah Beth could mean letting his past taint her life.

Toby's bat caught the ball, and it arched over the outfielders' heads. Elias joined in the cheering and soon was too busy enjoying the day to think about either the past or the future.

6

Though the first cutting of hay had already been stored in its upper level, the singing was to be held in the Waglers' bank barn. One section remained empty, leaving room for the next cutting, so there was enough room to set tables in a long row. Church benches were set on either side for the participants, males on one side and the females on the other. Seating was supposed to be random, but couples who were walking out together always seemed to find a way to sit across from each other. That way they could spend the time singing *and* flirting. The latter had to be done furtively. However, most couples considered the need to keep the "secret" part of the fun.

Married couples and families had taken their leave from the Waglers' farm earlier in order to get home in time to do barn chores. Elias had seen Toby head home with another lad around his age, but Sarah Beth and Cora were staying for the singing.

Was Sarah Beth there to spend time with other young folks, or did she intend to chaperone her sister? He guessed Sarah Beth was about twenty-four, which meant she was one of the oldest among those going to the youth event.

So what are you *doing hanging around with the kids? You're five years older than she is.*

He was beginning to despise the logical voice that taunted him whenever he let his guard down. The answer was simple. If he believed his assumption that the damage done to his shop might have begun as a youth prank, he needed to get to know the young people in the district. A group from a neighboring district was supposed to join them for the singing, and that would give him a chance to learn more about those on their *Rumspringa* in the area.

Though he'd been tempted to spend the whole afternoon with Sarah Beth while they watched the ball game and joined others to play volleyball, he'd spent time meeting other neighbors. He'd been glad that nobody asked about the vandalism to his shop. Keeping the incident quiet prevented the perpetrators from enjoying anonymous notoriety and, he hoped, would deter them. He knew too well how adult consternation could spur young men to try something more destructive and more dangerous.

As shadows lengthened, Elias watched the girls and young women go into the barn with refreshments for the first break in the singing. He drew in the scents of chocolate and apples. He wasn't sure if they carried apple cider or apple bars. Either way, it smelled delicious.

Sarah Beth emerged from the house, chatting with Edith Lehman. They carried trays of cookies, and Cora walked with them, balancing a stack of napkins and paper plates.

When Sarah Beth glanced in his direction, it was as if the evening grew warmer and the setting sun became as bright as midday. She smiled, mesmerizing him, before looking back at her friend and sister. Once her gaze didn't hold his, he could exhale and take another breath.

Wow! He hadn't expected a single smile from her to have such an overpowering effect on him. He should have, because he'd been thinking about Sarah Beth since he'd last spoken with her. When Toby came to assist him, Elias had to guard himself from talking too much about the boy's sister.

Stop it! he told himself. Before he'd moved to Hickory Meadows, he'd heard the rumors whispered about him and women, some he'd never met. Though the tales were untrue, by having her name attached to his, Sarah Beth's reputation could be damaged.

He should leave.

As Elias turned to do that, he heard someone call his name. He saw Darryl Glick, who stood with a half dozen other men, motioning to him. What could he want? That afternoon Darryl had spent all his time with Sarah Beth's friend Edith. Was Darryl anxious that the rumors about Elias were true? Elias realized the false rumors about him could hurt Sarah Beth's friend too.

Elias discovered that he'd misread the situation when Darryl greeted him with a grin. Darryl had a face filled with freckles to match his bright red hair. If he married Edith, they would have a house filled with carrot-topped Kinder.

"We've been admiring your buggy, Elias," Darryl said. "Is it new?"

He shook his head. "No. It's about ten years old. I rebuilt it."

"You rebuilt *this* buggy?" The man, whose name Elias hadn't caught when he was introduced before the church service, dropped onto his hands and knees and peered at the underside of the buggy. Standing, the man brushed dirt from his *Mutze's* hem and the knees of his black trousers. "It looks like new."

"Danki. We finished it yesterday."

"We? You've got a partner?" asked a boy a couple of years older than Toby.

"Not a partner. An apprentice," Elias answered.

"You aren't looking for another, are you?"

"Not yet. We don't have enough work yet for three." To ease the kid's disappointment, he added, "At this point, my apprentice isn't getting paid."

Questions were fired at him in quick succession from the other men, who were curious how he'd handled common problems with an aging buggy. He joined in the laughter and listened to other solutions and enjoyed the camaraderie as he hadn't been able to do in the past.

He relished the moment, glad that he'd chosen to move to Hickory Meadows. Catching a motion out of the corner of his eye, he saw Sarah Beth emerging from the barn. Ja, he was very glad he'd come to Hickory Meadows.

From where she stood by the refreshment table, Sarah Beth watched the other young women and girls waiting in the barn. They were getting annoyed that none of the guys had come in yet. The singing couldn't go late because everyone had early morning chores. For the girls, that meant making breakfast and starting the week's laundry. The men had to rise before dawn to do barn chores or catch a ride to their jobs. The longer the men stood outside, the less time the group would have for singing and chatting and flirting.

"When is Elias coming in?" whispered Cora, cupping her hand to keep others from hearing her.

Sarah Beth was pleased her sister had heeded her warning about revealing her "boyfriend." Patting Cora on the shoulder, she said, "Be patient."

"No one else is."

"If we are, they will be too."

"We're role models?"

"Ja." She fought her twitching lips that wanted to give in to a smile. "I'm going to be a *gut* role model."

"You already are."

Sarah Beth stepped aside as Edith set a sweating pitcher of lemonade on the table, then swiped condensation off her hands by slapping them together.

"That's the last of the lemonade," Edith said. "I brought it because I figured the rest would be gone by now. I didn't count on the guys acting like a bunch of Englisch teenagers when one of them gets a new car." She grinned. "As my Mamm says, 'Boys will be boys.'"

"No matter whether they're Englisch or plain."

They laughed, and Cora asked what was funny. After they'd explained, she chuckled too. The other young women wandered over and within minutes were giggling.

The sound must have reached the men outside because they appeared in the doorway. As they entered the barn, their shadows growing shorter behind them as they approached the propane lights set at the far end of the tables, the girls rushed to take their seats. Each wanted to give her beau a chance to see where she was so her guy would sit across from her.

Cora joined the stampede to the table, and Edith arched her brows.

"Go, go." Sarah Beth waved her hands. "You'll want to make sure someone special sits across from you."

Edith faced her. "I wish you had someone special too."

"I'll worry about that once the twins are home."

Her friend's eyes filled with tears, but Sarah Beth motioned for her to take her seat before someone else sat across from her Darryl. She watched as Elias sat next to Edith's fiancé and Cora slid into the spot across from him. Cora smiled and wiggled her fingers at him in a coquettish wave.

Going to the table, Sarah Beth put her hands on her sister's shoulders and bent to whisper, "Can you move slightly, Cora?"

"I want to sit with my . . ."

"You can sit here, but I need a bit more room to fit in beside you."

Cora shifted enough to leave Sarah Beth space on the bench. That allowed Cora to sit across from Elias while Sarah Beth faced the youngest Miller boy, who couldn't have been more than sixteen. Each time Sarah Beth looked at him, he blushed a bright crimson that swallowed every freckle scattered on his narrow face.

She imagined her brother at his first singing in a couple of years, when he was sixteen. Would he flush whenever a girl looked at him too?

Elias winked, and she had to grin. She hoped he wasn't disappointed to be sitting across from her and Cora when he could have been getting acquainted with other young women. After all, he'd spent most of the afternoon with her and her sister.

The thought unsettled her. She didn't want him to think she was looking for someone to walk out with. Not when she needed to focus every bit of her energy on getting the shop open so she could earn enough money to prove to her Aenti and Onkel that she could take care of her little sisters.

The young man chosen as the singing's *Vorsinger*, the one who led the singing, stood and began the first song. He was Edith's brother Fred. He had a pure voice and a *gut* set of lungs that allowed him to be heard over the other voices so they didn't lose the tempo of the hymn.

The time went more quickly than she'd expected. It was fun to sing the various songs, including the ones that became rounds or had parts only the guys sang and others for the girls. They didn't sing as slowly as during the church service, and more modern Christian songs were included. When Edith offered to teach them a new song she'd learned during a visit to another district, Sarah Beth was delighted to discover a new way to praise the Lord.

After the last song ended almost three hours later, at nine o'clock, Sarah Beth went to collect the empty pitchers and glasses and set them on the trays once covered with cookies and other treats. Only crumbs remained. She laughed when the boy who'd sat across from her snagged a few of those as he left.

Waste not, want not, she said to herself.

Edith had asked Sarah Beth and Cora to ride with her and Darryl to the Kings' farm. Sarah Beth appreciated her friend's sacrifice, because Sunday nights after singings were the sole times when Edith could spend time with her betrothed.

She heard her sister shout something that was muffled by the barn walls. Running into the darkness, she saw many buggies that were already leaving, taking the courting couples on the slow, roundabout way home.

Looking in every direction, she didn't see Cora until her sister's voice rang out in the sudden silence following her shout.

"No!" Cora cried to someone Sarah Beth couldn't identify in the dark. "Stay away from him! Elias is walking out with me, not with you."

Sarah Beth was grateful for the darkness because she was sure her face was bright red. It burned like an open flame as she rushed to where her sister was glowering at a quartet of startled girls. Putting her arm around Cora's slender shoulders, she discovered her sister was stiff with outrage.

"Remember?" Sarah Beth whispered. "Remember how we talked about letting the boy ask if he could take you home?"

"Oh!" Cora nodded so hard that her bonnet struck Sarah Beth on the nose.

Pain burst across her face, but she ignored the tears gathering in her eyes. She drew her sister to one side as the others paired off to go to their buggies.

Cora started to speak whenever one of the girls she'd lambasted came near, but each time Sarah Beth murmured a reminder to her.

Sarah Beth breathed a sigh of relief when the last of the four young women upsetting Cora departed. Her relief was short-lived when Sarah Beth realized Edith and Darryl had gone without them. Her best friend was never thoughtless, but she must have been so absorbed in Darryl's company that she'd forgotten about Sarah Beth and Cora needing a ride.

"Want to go home," Cora moaned, signaling that she, too, had noticed they'd been left behind.

"I know, dear." She kept her voice even because she didn't want to upset her sister further.

"Time to go home."

"I know."

"I want to go home *now*." Her sister had a one-track mind.

Sarah Beth considered their options. There weren't many. They could walk, but it was miles, and she doubted Cora had the energy for the journey after playing softball and volleyball and other games. They could ask the Waglers to let them stay or lend them a buggy.

"What's wrong?" asked Elias, appearing from the darkness.

Cora whirled and threw her arms around him, knocking him back a half step. "Oh, Elias, I'm glad we're walk—!" She clamped her lips closed.

"What's wrong?" he asked again. "Sarah Beth?"

"There was a mix-up," she said, trying to sound less distressed than she was. "Our ride left without us."

He chuckled. "That problem is easily solved. I'll take you and Cora home. Your house is on my way."

Before she answered, Sarah Beth sent Cora into the barn with instructions to return the metal trays to the Waglers' kitchen. The moment her sister was out of earshot, Sarah Beth said, "Danki, Elias, but this might cause more problems."

"What do you mean?"

"You taking us home might encourage Cora to believe you want to walk out with her."

"I haven't given her any reason to think we're more than friends."

"I know, but . . ." She looked at him for the first time, and her love for her sister battled with her *gut* sense.

In the faint light, she could see the lines of worry threading across his brow. He was as upset about her sister's potential reaction to his kind offer as she was.

She wondered why she was surprised. Elias watched over Toby, helping him learn and making sure he didn't get hurt around the heavy buggies and tools. Her brother acted as if he'd discovered a big brother, one who offered a male perspective that had been missing from Toby's life.

If Elias continued to treat her like a little sister, Cora would come to see him as Toby did. Her sister's affections changed on a whim.

"But?" prompted Elias.

"But nothing." She smiled and watched the lines ease on his forehead. "I fret too much about my siblings."

"I never would have guessed." He used just enough sarcasm to make her chuckle.

His words held up a mirror so she could see her overprotectiveness. If she wanted her sister to be more self-reliant—and she did—she had to give Cora room to make mistakes.

Knowing that, Sarah Beth withheld any comment when Cora climbed into the buggy and sat next to Elias. She didn't have a chance to slip a word in edgewise because Cora chatted all during the ride to the Kings' farm. Her excited sister asked Elias questions and didn't wait for him to reply as she continued to share her opinions about who'd said what during the singing. The fact that Sarah Beth and Elias had been present didn't seem to perturb Cora. She kept on talking.

Elias drew the buggy next to the well-weathered one Toby had driven home. Cora jumped down and headed toward the house.

"Aren't you going to say 'Danki' to Elias?" Sarah Beth called after her sister.

Not bothering to lower her voice, Cora replied, "I want to get inside before he thinks it's okay to kiss me. *Gut* girls have to careful, ain't so?"

Sarah Beth heard a smothered laugh as Elias walked around the buggy, but he didn't say anything as Cora opened the kitchen door. With a single glance at where Sarah Beth stood, Cora shut the door behind her, though Toby must still have been awake. Lights glowed from the windows.

"It doesn't do a man's ego much *gut* to have someone shout to the neighborhood that she's avoiding his kiss," Elias chuckled. "I have to say, Sarah Beth, your sister is one of a kind."

"She is." She was relieved he wasn't bothered by Cora's words and actions. "Do you want to sit?" She gestured toward the swing on the front porch, then wondered if she'd lost her mind. It wasn't as if they were walking out together, so she shouldn't be asking him to linger. Yet she felt obligated because he'd been nice enough to bring them home and endure her sister's antics.

If Elias was shocked by her invitation, she heard no sign of it in his voice. "Happily." He climbed the trio of steps. Taking the right-hand side of the swing, he propped his feet against the porch floor so it didn't move while she sat on the other side.

She was glad the swing had been built so wide. There was enough space between the two of them for one of the twins to join them. She'd been meaning to bring out the rockers they had taken inside during the winter, but she hadn't had time.

"I appreciate the ride," she said before the silence could settle over them.

"As I said," he replied with his easy smile that seemed to gleam in the faint light from the house, "your farm is on my way home."

"I am grateful, and Cora is too. Danki for not getting upset with her tonight."

"Why would I get upset?" His face showed honest surprise at her words. "Your sister might be outspoken, but a few girls at the singing tonight weren't much more circumspect once they set their eyes on a guy."

Sarah Beth smiled in spite of herself. "You're right. The guys aren't much subtler."

"Was Mahlon bothering you again?"

"Not enough to mention." It wasn't the truth, but she'd handle Mahlon as she had when they were younger and he'd tried to steal the dessert Grossmammi Miriam prepared for her school lunch.

She was confused by Mahlon's sudden interest in her. Since they'd finished school ten years ago, he hadn't said much to her. Why would he start flirting with her today?

As they rocked in unison on the swing, she pushed the thoughts from her head and tried to relax. She listened while Elias gave her an update on how much Toby had learned since he'd returned to helping at the buggy shop earlier in the week. The two had worked together well for the past five days. It wasn't a dry report, but one filled with humorous anecdotes. Not all were about Toby, because Elias seemed to have no problem with talking about his own goof-ups as they tried to bring an ancient buggy back to usable condition.

Sarah Beth couldn't be as honest about her mistakes. She struggled to be as perfect as possible while preparing to bring her younger sisters home. Anything she did wrong provided fodder for her Aenti and Onkel to insist the twins were better off with them.

Laughing along with Elias at a silly story about the extremes he and Toby had to go to in order to get the rusted wheels off the buggy, she found herself wondering what it would be like to have a handsome man like Elias bring her home in his courting buggy. Not because he was being kind but because he wanted to be alone with her.

They'd sit as they were on the porch, because a courting couple didn't hold hands in public until they were betrothed. Or would Elias be bold enough to put his arm along the back of the swing while they rocked together? Would his fingers curl down to caress her shoulder?

Her fantasy shattered when Elias stood. "I guess I should be going. Morning comes earlier every day this time of year."

"It does." She congratulated herself because her voice didn't tremble.

"*Gut Nacht*, Sarah Beth. I'll see you soon."

"*Gut* Nacht," she said, but he'd already started down the steps.

She didn't move while she watched him climb into his buggy and turn his horse toward the road. Only then did she stand. As the light from his buggy was swallowed by the night, leaving her only the stars for company, she knew she couldn't spend time on dreams of being courted by a nice man like Elias. She had one important dream, and she prayed that with God's help, it would come true.

And she'd be able to reunite her family forever.

7

The house where Sarah Beth's Aenti Neva and Onkel Bert lived was south of Ronks, fourteen miles north of Hickory Meadows. The heavily traveled roads in the center of Lancaster County were dangerous, and Sarah Beth's hands were shaking from her tight grip on the reins when later that week she turned into the driveway leading to their small brick house. It was a single story and built in a straight line, unlike the two-storied, rambling house with its attached *Dawdi Haus* where she lived.

The front door burst open, crashing against the brick, as Sarah Beth stepped from the buggy. She paused long enough to lash the reins around the hitching post. Turning, she held out her arms to her towheaded sisters. They threw theirs around her, almost knocking her off her feet.

She closed her eyes and savored embracing her youngest siblings. At twelve, they were, like Cora, a peculiar combination of child and teenager. Some days they considered themselves too mature to hug her. On others—*Danki, Lord, today is one of those days*—they were as affectionate and effusive as they'd been when they were toddlers.

It seemed impossible that only two years ago, Toby had acted as loving. Now he was a sullen fourteen-year-old, and she never could guess when he'd be too moody to do more than grunt in her and Cora's direction. He'd been less grumpy since he'd started working with Elias.

Holding Lovina and Luann away so she could examine them, Sarah Beth smiled. They were cute with their pale blonde hair and big brown eyes. On first glance, the twins looked identical, except that one of Luann's front teeth lapped over the edge of the one beside it. Sarah Beth had never been confused by their attempts to fool her when one pretended to be the other. Lovina had a few more freckles scattered across her nose and cheeks, and Luann's laugh was more musical. Small details, but enough for her to avoid letting them get away with mischief.

Sarah Beth smiled, wondering if they had any idea how much she and Toby and Cora missed them. "How are you doing?"

"All right," said Luann, unexpectedly, as Lovina usually answered first.

"Okay," added her twin.

"Just okay?" Sarah Beth asked.

"Okay is okay." Lovina grinned. "Ain't so?"

"Apparently so." Sarah Beth savored the moment because the twins didn't seem impatient to be done talking to her and eager to get away to do something with their friends.

As she turned to walk toward the house, the girls stayed where they were.

Sarah Beth paused and asked, "What is it?"

Both girls giggled.

"What is it?" she asked again. "What have you two cooked up?"

"We want to go to Hickory Meadows," Luann said.

Sarah Beth's heart did a flip-flop in her chest, leaving her breathless. The twins were asking to come home? Her first burst of happiness faded as she wondered what had caused this abrupt change of heart. She cautioned herself. Preteens were as subject to mood swings as teens, and their request could be nothing but a whim.

"It'd be nice to have you come home," she said.

"We want to see Elias's shop." Lovina glanced at her twin. "Ja, we want to see the shop."

"What?" Sarah Beth couldn't imagine any request that would have amazed her more. "You want to go to a buggy shop? Why?"

Luann's smile broadened. "Because Toby told us about it when he and Cora stopped by a couple of days ago. He's really excited about working there."

Sarah Beth hadn't known her brother and sister had paid the twins a call. How had she missed that? Toby might keep things close to his chest, but Cora usually couldn't hold on to a secret.

Luann continued, "We want to see it too."

"Ja, Toby is excited, but it's because he . . ." Sarah Beth halted herself, not wanting to drag the twins into her ongoing argument with their brother about finishing his chores before going to the shop. So instead she said, "Because he likes learning about buggies."

"He's told us what he's been doing to fix a buggy and what he's learned from Elias. Toby would love for us to come." Lovina looked at her twin, who nodded.

"Can we?" Luann asked.

"We want to meet Elias too. Toby says he's a *gut* guy. He might let us help."

"Toby?" Sarah Beth tried to sort out her sisters' sudden interest in a buggy shop.

"No!" Luann giggled. "Elias."

"We should meet him if he's walking out with Cora."

Sarah Beth halted herself from rolling her eyes as Cora had. She hoped her sister hadn't spoken of her imaginary courtship in front of their Onkel and Aenti. Letting her sister become involved with a man would be another black mark against Sarah Beth in their eyes.

"Can we go?" Lovina asked, her large brown eyes wide.

Sarah Beth considered how long it would take to drive home and then turn around and bring them back. A pulse of excitement raced through her. The girls' beds were made with fresh linen, waiting for them to return. Why not tonight?

"You don't have any other plans for the afternoon and evening?" Sarah Beth was glad no hint of her anxiety that they would change their mind slipped into her voice.

"No!" both girls answered at the same time, then giggled more.

Sending up a prayer of gratitude, Sarah Beth said, "I don't see any reason why you shouldn't go and see the buggy Toby has been working on." She raised one hand. "I need to let Aenti and Onkel know that you'll be gone overnight."

"Will you ask them, Sarah Beth?" asked Luann.

"If you want me to."

The twins exchanged glances, and this time Sarah Beth was able to guess its meaning. Neither girl wanted to ask. Sensing how reluctant their relatives would be to let them go was a sign the twins were growing up.

Sarah Beth wasn't going to let this opportunity pass. She would have preferred to avoid a confrontation, but that had kept the twins away for two years. With her plans for the shop coming together, she hoped to begin work on it soon. Once it opened, she'd be able to provide for her sisters without cutting corners elsewhere.

Telling the twins to go to their room and be ready to pack their bags, Sarah Beth went into the house. She heard voices from the kitchen, which wasn't a surprise. Aenti Neva spent every day in there, except when she was cleaning or doing laundry. Dust would die of loneliness in the pristine house, something that couldn't be said for the Kings' farmhouse.

"I thought I heard your buggy," Aenti Neva said from beside the stove. She was stirring a steaming pot that smelled like chicken and dumplings. A few strands of graying hair hung along her plump cheeks, but her blue eyes were welcoming.

"Told you," said Onkel Bert in his gruff voice. "Told you it was Sarah Beth coming. Are you staying for supper?"

"Actually," Sarah Beth said, "the girls would like to visit Hickory Meadows."

Her Aenti dropped her spoon against the pot with a sharp clang. Turning to face Sarah Beth, she shot a look at her husband before she asked, "For how long? One night?" Aenti Neva bit her lower lip before saying, "I don't know if. . ."

Was she hesitating to try to devise an excuse why the twins shouldn't go to Hickory Meadows?

Sarah Beth would never know because Onkel Bert smiled. "I think it's a *gut* idea."

"Bert . . . ," began her Aenti.

"Neva," he said, "the girls have been pining for their sisters and brother. A visit will ease their unhappiness. It's only one night."

"Is it?" Aenti Neva scanned Sarah Beth's face as if looking for a sign of dishonesty.

Sarah Beth forced herself not to bristle at her Aenti's reaction, which suggested that a hideous kidnapping was about to take place. Despair dropped on her like a heavy wool blanket as she realized she now had the proof of what she'd long suspected: Aenti Neva didn't want to let the twins rejoin their siblings in Hickory Meadows.

"I wouldn't want them to be away from school any longer," Sarah Beth replied.

Her Aenti frowned again, recalling that there was a school in Hickory Meadows too. "I hope you're prepared to take care of them overnight."

"I raised them until they came here," Sarah Beth said, trying not to let annoyance slip into her words.

Sarah Beth didn't give her time to change her mind. Calling an enthusiastic "Danki," she rushed to the girls' room. When she told them the good news, they grabbed their bags, which were already packed. That warned her that her sisters were well aware of their Aenti's well-meaning intentions to keep the family separated.

Opening the shop couldn't happen soon enough.

After stopping at the farm to collect Cora and leave the twins' bags in their bedroom, Sarah Beth drove her sisters across the covered bridge to Elias's shop. The weather was ideal, with a light breeze and glorious sunshine. The day would have seemed perfect, though, even if the temperature were hovering around freezing and the sky filled with low, ominous clouds.

She and all her sisters were together, the four of them enjoying a short ride past freshly planted fields and meadows where cows grazed. They waved to their neighbors, both plain and Englisch.

Cora was thrilled to see the twins. Her sisters chattered like a trio of magpies. She wondered if they were listening to what the other was saying; then she realized it didn't matter. They were—as she was—filled with joy at being together.

When Sarah Beth drew Cinnamon to a stop in front of the buggy shop, the younger girls skipped ahead, impatient to see inside. Cora grabbed each one by the hand and joined them.

Sarah Beth let a contented sigh ease past her smile. How *wunderbar* to have her youngest sisters with them!

In some ways, she was more like their Mamm than their sister. It was too bad she wasn't. If the twins had been her Bopplin, they wouldn't have been taken away. A plain community supported every member in it, and she and the rest of her family would have been taken care of until they could manage on their own.

Or would her Bopplin have been taken from her as the twins had been? It was true that she and the rest of her siblings didn't have much money, and what they had must be put into the farm—and now into the shop—to work toward their future. With their financially well-established Onkel and Aenti, her sisters never had to worry about slim pickings at the supper table.

Everything would change once the shop was completed and Sarah Beth could begin selling her birdhouses and other items there. She'd be able to provide everything the twins needed, and they would be a true family again.

Tonight, after supper, she'd ask the girls to help her paint blank birdhouses. She remembered the whimsical drawings they used to make before they went to live in Ronks.

As she followed them toward Elias's shop, she pictured bringing her own Kinder to a shop not so different from this one. Their Daed would work hard to give them what they needed . . . and something special for their birthdays or a Christmas present.

Sarah Beth shook her head to banish the thoughts. Why was she thinking of a distant someday that might never happen? She wanted to relish this time with her whole family together.

When she entered the shop, she heard the twins greeting their brother and Toby's excited replies. Her gaze didn't focus on that happy sight, however. Instead she looked at Elias, who was picking up something from the floor. Her eyes locked with his as he stood.

His face lit up with his smile. His eyes glowed, making her feel she was the most special person in the whole world. In *his* whole world. For the briefest moment, happiness rocketed through her; then her breath caught as she realized he was standing in the middle of what looked like debris.

Tearing her gaze from his, she looked around the buggy shop. She clasped her hands in front of her chest and stared in disbelief. Tools were scattered everywhere, as they'd been when his shop was vandalized. It had happened again. It was worse this time because someone had taken the lubricants he used on the axles and wheels and splashed them across the back wall. Shining lines of oil emphasized every uneven surface.

The two buggies in the shop had suffered worse damage. Green, gray, and black paint had been sprayed on their sides.

She struggled to find something to say, but the only word she found was "Why?"

Elias wished he had an answer for Sarah Beth's question. Since he'd walked into his shop after meeting with his landlord and running errands in town, including a stop at Yoder's Store, he'd tried to guess why anyone would want to damage his shop.

Again.

His past wasn't known to anyone around Hickory Meadows. Even if it had been, he couldn't see how it would lead to vandalism.

"I don't know," he replied when he realized he'd left her waiting for a response. "I . . ."

His eyes widened when he saw two girls who were miniatures of Sarah Beth. *They must be the King twins.*

He realized he'd guessed right when his apprentice draped his arms around their shoulders. They looped theirs around him as he hugged them and lifted them off their feet. Cora was grinning as they watched, and Sarah Beth lost her expression of despair for a moment as Toby and the girls began to tease each other.

The connection between the Kings was strong, and the dark shadow of envy roiled in Elias's gut. For as long as he could remember, he'd wanted a family. That longing hadn't eased when he'd been left behind by relatives and strangers who had never let him into their homes without first reminding him he was an uninvited burden. Would it have been different if there had been someone like Sarah Beth in his life? Someone determined to make a family from the remnants of one torn apart by loss?

It was another question he couldn't answer, so Elias smiled when Toby introduced his younger sisters, and they giggled as they looked at him.

Elias realized that although on first glance they looked like Sarah Beth, they had Toby's brown eyes. They were going to be beauties. He hoped Sarah Beth was prepared to deal with three teenagers instead of one.

"This is my boyfriend," Cora announced, motioning toward him. "Elias and I are walking out—" She clamped her hand over her mouth and shot a guilty glance toward Sarah Beth.

"Elias is our friend as well as our neighbor." Sarah Beth's tone suggested the topic was closed.

Wanting to thank her for not letting the twins get the wrong idea, Elias said, "Ja. I'm glad to have *gut* neighbors."

"We're *gut* neighbors," Cora agreed with a big grin. "*Gut* neighbors help each other, so we'll help you."

"That we will." Sarah Beth didn't let him protest but gave quiet orders to her siblings.

The four scattered to obey, the twins delighted to work with their brother and sisters. Elias heard water running after Toby vanished outside, and the girls found push brooms in a cupboard. Soon the Kings were working to redd up the mess as if the shop were theirs.

"Danki," Elias said as he moved closer to Sarah Beth and continued to pick up the tools that had been tossed everywhere.

"Cora is right. We want to be *gut* neighbors." She had a bucket of soapy water and was trying to clean the slippery walls with a long-handled brush he hadn't known he had.

"I wasn't talking about your help, though I appreciate that."

She gave him a faint grin. Lowering her voice, she said, "As far as Cora, treat her as you would the twins. Cora is, at heart, like them. As you've noticed, she can't hide how she feels, and she says what she thinks."

"I've noticed none of you Kings seem to have a problem speaking your minds."

He immediately knew he'd chosen the wrong words. Sarah Beth's eyes widened in astonishment before her expression closed like a slammed door.

"I'm sorry, Sarah Beth. I didn't mean it as it sounded."

"It's okay. I know *you* didn't. I'm a little off-kilter today."

He wanted to ask her who or what had upset her, but she bent to her task. The motion was a clear indicator she'd said all she intended to on that subject.

When she asked him if he had any ideas of who was wrecking his shop, he said, "I don't know many people in Hickory Meadows yet. I've met the Leit in our district, but that's about it other than Harry Fitzgerald."

Her head jerked up. "You think Harry had something to do with this?" She dunked the scrub brush into the pail and squeezed it, leaving the water a peculiar green shade. "Why would he do damage to his own building?"

"He's been persistent about getting me to move."

"It *is* his building, though." Her nose wrinkled as she regarded the filthy wall. "I can't imagine him doing something like this."

Elias couldn't either, so he went to work putting his tools and supplies where they belonged. That allowed him time to think too much, so he returned to his worktable and the dashboard he'd been working on earlier. He needed to focus on a task to keep his mind from filling with contradictory theories.

He looked around as he listened to the Kings talking and laughing as they worked together. It was clear they considered the idea of work frolic to mean exactly that. Working *and* having a *gut* time. He could see clearly that they were a family who loved one another. Toby might push against his older sister's expectations, but he was the first one to volunteer to get her a fresh bucket of water. The twins peppered him with questions about buggies, as eager to learn as their brother.

As the sun dropped toward the western horizon, Elias wasn't surprised when Sarah Beth announced that the King siblings needed to return to the farm to do evening chores. Her brother and sisters seemed relieved to be done, though there was a lot remaining to do.

"Danki for your help," he said, wishing he could express the true gratitude in his heart.

For a few minutes, as he'd worked and laughed along with them, he'd felt as if he were a part of their family. It was a precious gift, though he suspected they didn't realize what they'd done beyond redding up.

"We're glad to help," Sarah Beth said with a smile that made his heart skip as the twins raced Cora to the family's buggy. "Danki for answering all the questions Lovina and Luann asked. They are as curious as a whole litter of kittens."

"And as cute."

She smiled. "I think so too, though they've got a streak of mischief as wide as Toby's. What one doesn't think up, the other does. They've always kept me on my toes, but I'm so happy to have them with us tonight that I don't care."

"And I'm happy that you're letting Toby work for me. He absorbs information as fast as I can share it. I seldom have to show him how to do a task twice, which gives me time to work on the more complicated parts of rebuilding the buggy."

"Danki for letting me know." Her grin was so bright it could have illuminated a building twice the size of the shop.

"Before you go," he said, knowing he'd dim her bright spirits and sorry he had to, "I wanted to tell you something."

"What?"

He watched her face. "I went to look at the place near Strasburg with Harry today."

Her expression didn't change, but he saw a flash of strong emotion in her eyes. "Are you moving there?"

"No. Despite what Harry said, the space wouldn't work as well for me as this place does." He pushed on before he lost his nerve. "I didn't like the neighbors as well."

"You don't know them."

"I don't have to." He sandwiched her hand between his much larger ones. "I couldn't like them as much as I do the Kings."

A blush deepened the pink in her cheeks, and he wondered if he'd ever seen anything more beautiful than that color on her lovely face. It was a sight he could savor for hours on end.

"We like having you as our neighbor too." She drew her fingers from under his. She spun on her heel and walked to the door, herding her brother ahead of her. He was shocked when she turned and asked, "Do you want to join us for supper?"

"But the twins are home with you."

"We do something special when they're eating with us. If you're curious what, why don't you come and see?" Her eyes sparkled like the light of the setting sun off the windows.

"Danki. I'll do that."

"See you then."

She left him grinning like a fool. Going to the door, he watched the family climb into the buggy. He waved as the buggy drove toward their farm.

Shutting the back door, he searched for the key that should have been hanging nearby. His happiness tempered as he found it, locked the door, and then pocketed the key. He'd never thought he'd have to secure the door on his shop.

Why had his shop been targeted? Nobody knew him well enough to want to do him harm.

His eyes widened. Maybe the beef wasn't with him but with Harry Fitzgerald. If someone wanted to hurt Harry, the easiest way would be to do damage to his bottom line. Elias might be an innocent bystander.

He snorted a laugh. Innocent? Nobody had believed that about him for so many years he no longer believed it himself. He couldn't imagine anyone ever would. If he wanted to find who was behind the damage, he would have to keep looking.

On his own.

8

Elias whistled a light tune that echoed within the covered bridge. The day had started out rough, but he was grateful that God had used Sarah Beth to bring feelings of family and community into his life. Was it gratitude he felt or something much stronger? The thought of seeing Sarah Beth made his heart beat faster.

Pausing as he reached the end of the Kings' farm lane, Elias looked at two new birdhouses added to the display of items for sale on the farm stand's narrow wooden shelves. On a tall, narrow birdhouse, Sarah Beth had painted flowers in blue and yellow that twisted along its white sides. The other was a four-story house for purple martins. It had a deep-green roof and white walls. Three entrances were visible on each side, offering plenty of space for the small birds' nests. The red stripe over each opening displayed the words *Home Sweet Home* in tiny letters, and there were painted doormats in front. Each of the welcome mats was unique.

He admired Sarah Beth's imagination as well as her clever knowledge of what would appeal to Englisch tourists. The birdhouses wouldn't go unsold long. In fact, he thought one might look *gut* near his shop. It would be eye-catching, drawing attention to his business.

His smile faded as he strode up the dirt road toward the house. He'd prefer *less* attention to the shop. Nothing he'd seen in the mess gave him any clue as to who'd done the damage or why. Was it more than youthful pranks? Was someone trying to drive him away from Hickory Meadows? If others had learned about his past, they might not want him in the area.

Joyous greetings met Elias, wiping away his dreary thoughts, when he opened the door, though an hour hadn't passed since he'd watched the Kings drive away from his shop. Luann and Lovina rushed to him before he could discover where Sarah Beth was. Each twin grabbed his hand before leading him to the table. With more of what seemed to be their endless supply of giggles, they handed him a black apron.

"What am I supposed to do with this?" he asked as he saw Sarah Beth by the stove. She was overseeing something in a pot. Something with Italian spices, his nose told him.

"Put it on," answered the twin he was pretty sure was Luann. "If you want to eat on pizza night, you have to work."

"You need to warn a man so he knows what he's getting himself into when he accepts an invitation to supper."

Sarah Beth continued to stir more spices into the pot on the stove. The enticing aromas of oregano and basil floated through the kitchen. "You need to ask more questions before you accept an invitation to supper."

At her pert retort, her siblings roared with laughter.

Toby motioned for Elias to stand beside him. The girls had claimed the other side of the table. Flour was spread across the top, and the twins and Cora cheered when Sarah Beth set small mixing bowls in front of them.

Elias looked at her as she placed one by him as well. "What am I supposed to do with a bowl of dough?"

She laughed as she tipped the bowl and let the soft dough ooze onto the flour. "You're supposed to make your share of supper."

"Biscuits?"

His question set off a new round of giggles from the girls, and Toby guffawed as if he'd asked the silliest thing in the history of mankind.

"It's pizza dough," the boy said between laughs.

Sarah Beth took pity on him, saying as she walked to the stove, "Elias, welcome to pizza night. On pizza night, we each make our own little pies by topping them with whichever ingredients we like best. Once they're cooked, we share them."

"What if someone doesn't want to help?"

She raised her wooden spoon and tapped it on the side of the pot. "If someone doesn't help, that person doesn't get to eat any of our delicious pizza."

He winked at the twins. "Well, I'm not going to let that happen!"

The girls showed him how to put oil on his fingers before he began to stretch the ball of dough into something resembling a circle. Again, as when they'd worked together at the shop, he was suffused with a feeling of belonging to a real family. The Kings were a family, even when they were separated.

Pretending to be more helpless in the kitchen than he actually was, he delighted the twins and Cora—and Toby—as they "assisted" him with his pizza. They cheered when Sarah Beth brought homemade sauce to the table and ladled the proper amount on top of the round, flat pieces of dough. Elias teased the twins by pretending to put onions on their sauce after they told him how they despised onions on pizza.

Once each pizza was completed with a thick topping of shredded cheese and more spices, Sarah Beth sent her sisters into the bathroom to wash their hands while Toby went to use the sink in the barn. Elias smiled when he saw one twin slip from the house to follow her brother.

"Lovina loves seeing the animals," Sarah Beth explained as she placed each pie onto half of a cookie sheet. "She doesn't get much chance at our Onkel and Aenti's house because they don't have any except their buggy horse."

"Do you have other traditions like pizza night?" Elias asked, stepping aside so she could slide a hand under his pizza.

"Plenty."

"I appreciate you sharing this one with me."

"It's a night to celebrate." She glanced at the bathroom where the sound of splashing water could be heard.

If she was upset about the mess Luann might be making, she showed no sign. He realized she was thrilled to have her whole family under one roof and would have indulged her siblings with anything.

"There," she said with a smile.

He watched as she admired their handiwork. Six small pizzas were arranged, two by two, on the cookie sheets. There were two with pepperoni, two with mushrooms and onions, one with bacon bits, and one—the last one—with no toppings other than sauce and cheese. She'd put it together after she'd made sure everyone else had everything they needed.

"What now?" he asked.

"Now they cook." She took a dishrag and used it to hold onto the pans without getting any oil from her hands on them. She put them into the oven before she glanced at the clock. "Fifteen minutes, and we'll feast."

"Where?" He looked at the flour-covered table.

She laughed. "Redding up is part of the fun of cooking. Don't you know that, Elias?"

"Can't say I do, but then most of what I eat comes from a can."

Tossing him a dry cloth, she pointed at the trash basket. "Brush the loose flour into that, and I'll wash the table." She laughed. "Get to work if you want to enjoy your supper."

It took longer than he'd expected to have the oak table glistening again, and the floor would need to be swept where flour had fallen. He was about to offer when he heard the kitchen faucet come on as Sarah Beth began to rinse her dishrag and hands at the same time.

"This is the part," she said with a grimace as she rubbed her hands together hard, "I don't like. When it's dry, flour flies everywhere. When it's wet, it sticks to everything. But when it's been wet and dries, it's like concrete."

He walked over to stand behind her. His long arms reached around her. As he slipped his hands under the tap and began to peel the sticky dough off her fingers, she tried to jerk them away.

"Don't be skittish," he murmured so his voice wouldn't reach the others. "I'm trying to help."

"Is that what you're trying to do?"

He grinned. "It's what I'm trying to do. Help, though I've got to say for a woman who works as hard as you do, you've got soft hands."

"That's the olive oil."

"Can you be less practical for a moment?"

The question must have surprised her, because she froze. Her blue eyes were wide as she turned and gazed at him. Her lips, he noticed, were at the perfect angle beneath his for a kiss.

He couldn't think of anything but finding out if her lips were as luscious as they appeared. If he drew in his arms, they'd slip around her slender form, bringing her against him.

The back door opened, and Toby and his sister burst in, talking up a storm.

Sarah Beth ducked beneath Elias's right arm and away from him. He fought his yearning to give chase and pull her to his chest as he explored every inch of her pretty lips. Throughout the meal, which he assumed was delicious because Sarah Beth's siblings raved about the pizza, he couldn't think of anything else but holding her. The way she avoided looking at or speaking to him suggested her thoughts matched his.

Did the thought of being in his arms please her or make her want to run in the opposite direction? He should be honest with her about the man he'd been before he came to Hickory Meadows.

But then she might keep as much space between them as possible, and he wasn't sure if his badly patched heart could tolerate being shattered again.

"Elias!"

Toby's shout echoed through the barn as he poked his head past the front door and yelled again.

"Back here!" Elias called as he closed and locked the rear door.

What was the boy doing at the shop at this hour? The sky was barely lit in the east, and the brightest stars still twinkled along the western horizon. Toby should be in the Kings' cow barn, milking. Or he should be having breakfast with his sisters.

Elias thought about the meal he'd enjoyed with the Kings. A week had passed since he'd shared their laughter while they'd made pizzas together. He couldn't remember another evening he'd enjoyed as much. The Kings had made him feel as if he were a vital part of their pizza night.

And Sarah Beth . . .

He'd been brazen to help her wash her hands, but the memory of her smooth skin had remained with him. It dominated his waking thoughts and snuck into his dreams. Every attempt he'd made to push it away, reminding himself he didn't deserve a wunderbar woman like Sarah Beth King, only seemed to make the memory return stronger.

Toby rushed toward him, then stopped. Leaning forward, he put his hands on his legs and gasped for breath. Had the boy run all the way from the farm? Toby's shoes were soaked, and Elias realized he'd waded the creek to get to the buggy shop more quickly.

"What's wrong?" Elias asked.

"The farm stand . . ." Toby gulped and drew in a deep breath.

"What's happened to the farm stand?"

"I'm not sure, but Sarah Beth said to come quick."

Elias ignored the questions erupting through his mind as he grabbed the boy by the arm and steered him out of the shop. "Get in," he ordered, hooking his thumb toward his buggy, which he'd had ready to drive to a meeting with a potential customer first thing that morning.

Barely giving the boy a chance to climb in, Elias slapped the reins on the horse and turned it toward the Kings' farm. He asked Toby questions, but the boy didn't have many answers.

Toby had been milking when Sarah Beth burst in and told him to go and get Elias. She hadn't said anything else, but Toby guessed something was wrong with the farm stand. He hadn't been able to see it as he raced across the fields.

Elias slapped the reins harder on Wonder Boy, the name the retired racer had when he got him. As if the horse had been waiting for the opportunity to stretch out again, the buggy took off at a wild pace. Elias reined in the horse as they bounced over the rough boards in the covered bridge.

"Wow!" Toby crowed. "He can move."

"Not fast enough, because he was sold at auction."

Toby didn't answer, and Elias understood why when he slowed the buggy near what remained of Sarah Beth's farm stand. The boy jumped out, but Elias had to force his legs to move. His feet felt numb as they touched the ground. He stared at the destruction in front of him.

The boy's explanation that something had happened at the farm hadn't hinted at the extent of the damage. The simple structure had been annihilated. Debris was scattered through the field between the road and the house. All that remained of the farm stand were shattered pieces of wood. He saw broken baskets peeking from beneath the boards along with what might have been the corner of a quilt. It was difficult to tell because the fabric had been ground into the mud.

In the midst of the devastation, Sarah Beth held a flashlight and was directing its beam on the ground. With her other hand she picked through the split and broken sections of wood. Cora stood beside her with a plastic laundry basket. When Sarah Beth found something worth saving, she pulled it from the muddy ruts left by what appeared to be tires. She flicked the muck off before placing the item in the basket as if it were a person who'd been run over by a car and needed her tender care.

Elias walked toward them. His toe struck a small basket that skittered off into the shadows.

"I'll get it," Toby said.

Sarah Beth looked up at the sound of her brother's voice, and Elias guessed she hadn't noticed their arrival. She'd been so intent on her search for what could be salvaged.

Though the light was faint, he could see her expression. It was one he'd never thought to see on her face. Defeat. Though he was sure she would bounce back—as Sarah Beth always seemed to—this morning must have been one of the toughest in her life.

He said, "I'm sorry, Sarah Beth."

"Danki." Her voice was as dull as her eyes.

"Elias, find the bad people who did this," Cora pleaded.

"It could have been an accident." The protest was automatic, but he could see none of the Kings believed his words. No surprise—he didn't either. He'd merely wanted to offer comfort.

That wasn't the way to do it. Like Cora, he had to be forthright and not skirt the difficult truth that someone must have driven a vehicle into the farm stand. There was no other explanation for how far some pieces of wood had been thrown.

They worked in silence, saving what they could. Which wasn't much.

When his curiosity got the best of him, he asked, "Have you found the purple martins' house?"

"It sold yesterday." Sarah Beth knelt and pushed aside a board, then gave a soft cry. She cradled her right hand in her left.

"Are you okay?"

"Ja. It's just a splinter."

"Let me see."

She placed her injured hand on his palm, startling him. He hadn't been sure she'd let him touch her—even so he could help her—again.

Gently he tilted her hand until he could see the pinprick of blood on her index finger. Having her hold her flashlight steady, he plucked the splinter from beneath her skin.

"You're *gut* at that," she said in amazement.

"I've had lots of experience from years of working with wood and getting plenty of slivers in my fingers."

She covered her face with her hands and began to weep.

Cora threw her arms around her. "Bad people make Sarah Beth sad."

Sarah Beth sent her sister to help Toby look through the broken farm stand. As Cora obeyed, Sarah Beth looked at Elias. Tracks of tears had cut silvery paths along her cheeks, and more glistened in her eyes.

Elias wanted to drop to his knees beside her and comfort her. Before he could move, she stood and threw herself against him. His arms surrounded her slender warmth as she wept on his shirt.

He wished he had the words to make everything better, but there were none. She was frustrated and hurt and desperate to know why someone would destroy her livelihood.

Exactly how he'd felt each time his buggy shop was vandalized.

Waiting in silence, he held her close. He tried not to act as if each sob was a knife cutting into him.

When Sarah Beth stopped crying, she pushed herself away. He let her go, though doing so was one of the hardest things he'd ever done. Having her in his arms was sweet . . . or it would have been if under other circumstances. She started to apologize but halted when Toby shouted for Elias to come over to where he squatted. He waved his arms to emphasize his words.

Elias saw Toby's fingers hovering over a muddy rut. As they got closer, Toby cautioned him to be careful where he stepped.

"Look!" Toby exclaimed. "It's a footprint."

Elias motioned the boy to move aside so he could examine what Toby had discovered. More light shone from the eastern sky with each passing minute. One glance was enough for him to see that the boy was right. It was a footprint. There was a trail of what appeared to be sneaker prints across the soft ground.

"Yours?" Elias asked.

Toby held up his foot. "It's a different pattern than mine." He glanced at Elias's feet. "You're wearing work boots. They can't be ours."

"Or your sisters'. Their feet are much smaller."

"Do you think whoever ran into the farm stand got out and walked around?" *To see what damage they'd done* was the unspoken part of Toby's question.

Elias stood and wiped his hands, though he hadn't gotten mud on them. Something felt disgusting about the whole incident. The damage looked intentional.

"We have to assume whoever made these footprints is connected to the vehicle that dug those ruts in the grass." He rubbed his hands against the sides of his trousers. "The prints don't tell us who was in the car. Both Englischers and plain folks wear sneakers."

"Only Englischers drive cars," Toby said.

"That's not true. Some young people learn to drive during their Rumspringa to see what it's like or to enjoy the speed." Elias crossed his arms on his chest and glared at the footprints. "It could have been kids joyriding."

"If that was the case, they didn't have the decency to come to the house and explain what had happened."

"True."

When the boy headed toward the barn to begin the morning chores, Elias walked to where Sarah Beth and Cora were beginning to pile the broken lumber to one side of the farm lane. He was glad whoever had struck the farm stand hadn't gone to the house. The driver could have been intoxicated, and he didn't like the idea of Sarah Beth answering the door in the middle of the night and finding a drunk on the other side.

When she dropped another board on top of the growing stack, he asked, "Did you hear anything, Sarah Beth?"

"I heard a few cars going by during the night," she replied, knocking dried mud off her hands. "They slow down in front of the house when they see the covered bridge ahead of them." She frowned. "I did hear a buggy go by really late. They're loud as they go through the covered bridge, and when it's quiet, I can hear metal wheels on the uneven boards."

"You didn't hear something smash into your farm stand?"

She shook her head. "I must have been in a deep sleep."

"I heard," Cora interjected.

Sarah Beth asked, "You did? What did you hear?"

"Something went crash. Three times."

Elias glanced at the broken boards. What Cora was saying made sense. Judging by the harm done to the farm stand and the various angles where the boards had landed, it had been had struck more than once.

"Cora," he asked, "did you happen to see what time it was when you heard the noise?"

"It was dark, and my flashlight was downstairs." She glanced at Sarah Beth. "I forgot and left it in the bathroom."

Sarah Beth patted her arm. "Try to remember it next time so you don't fall if you have to come downstairs before daylight." With a smile, she asked, "Will you help Toby with the milking? The cows don't like to wait."

Her sister nodded and hurried toward the barn.

Sarah Beth's smile fell away. "This was deliberate."

"I want to tell you you're wrong, but I can't." His mouth tightened as he added, "Look at the boards. They're twisted in both directions. Someone drove into the farm stand and then backed up over it."

"That doesn't mean it wasn't an accident. Whoever was driving might have struck it by mistake and panicked."

"If I hadn't been dealing with damage at my shop, I'd agree with you."

Sarah Beth found it hard to breathe. "You think the damage to your shop and this destruction are related, Elias?"

"Anyone could have witnessed you last week bringing the twins to help me and Toby at the shop. Several vehicles drove past while you were there, and you might have been seen on your way here."

"Why does that matter? We were being neighborly. Anyone in Hickory Meadows would have done the same."

"Not everyone." He swallowed hard as his gaze swept the jumble of boards again. "Are you going to rebuild?"

"Ja, but not here. I'd already planned to open a shop."

"A full shop? Where?"

She pointed to the small building in the shadows cast by the main barn. "There. Edith and Cora and I have been clearing it out. I'm going to open a shop there so I can have more merchandise to sell to tourists. It's close to the house, and I'll have a view of it from the kitchen. When customers come, I'll wait on them."

"Closer to the house might be a *gut* idea."

A shiver drew an icy finger down her spine. Elias wasn't trying to frighten her more, and she appreciated his insight, but she couldn't wrap her mind around the idea of someone destroying her farm stand because she and her family had helped him redd up his shop. The idea that the attack on his shop and the one at the farm were related scared her to her marrow. She didn't know what to think. She'd been the victim of vandalism before Elias's arrival. But all of this seemed different somehow.

"Do you have any idea who might have done this?" she asked, torn between hoping he knew and not wanting to believe someone in their community had done the damage.

"None." He pushed back his hat and wiped his brow on his arm. "How are you going to display your merchandise in your new shop?"

"There are a couple of tables in the attic I can use."

"I'll build you shelves and new tables if you want." He glanced at the barn where light glowed in the windows of the milking parlor. "Toby and I will. A buggy maker needs to work with wood as well as metal. Do you have paint for the interior of your shop?"

"Some." New tears welled in her eyes, but these were tears of happiness and relief at his generous offer.

"*Gut*! We'll paint it for you." Elias grinned. "Knowing how to paint is also a vital skill in my business, so that will give me a chance to see how well Toby does with a brush. I'm sure you'll agree it's easier to fix mistakes on a wall than on someone's buggy."

"If you're offering to do this to keep your eyes on us, it's not necessary."

"I won't argue whether it's necessary or not. I want to see how well Toby paints and uses woodworking tools."

When he smiled, she had to exert her strength to keep from throwing her arms around him again and giving him a huge hug. Having his brawny arms envelope her would close out the rest of the world, and she could lose herself within his embrace while she forgot the troubles stalking her.

No! she told herself. She couldn't forget something far more important than a busted farm stand: getting her sisters home. After their short visit last week, she ached to have them home for *gut*. Her Onkel might be convinced, but when Sarah Beth had taken her sisters back to Ronks, Aenti Neva had hurried the twins into the house as if she were afraid Sarah Beth would snatch them and not bring them back. She hadn't given Sarah Beth a chance to say goodbye to them.

"Danki, Elias," she said when she was sure her voice was steady. "Having you help would be wunderbar." Inspiration burst into her head. "Wait here, will you? I'll be right back."

Elias stared. What had sent her flying toward the house as if she were as young as her twin sisters? She was going to return, or so she said.

While he waited, he continued the work she and Cora had begun. Little of the wood from the farm stand would be reusable. Dried by winter winds and summer sunshine, it had snapped like kindling.

He sighed, not wanting this destruction to be connected to his shop's. Sarah Beth and her family had been so *gut* to him, and he didn't like to think she was collateral damage to whomever had vandalized the buggy shop.

"Here!" Sarah Beth's lilting voice caught his attention. She was back, holding a tall, narrow birdhouse out to him.

He grinned when he saw the Red Sox logo on it. Bright red socks with white heels and toes displayed atop a baseball had been painted on one side of the birdhouse.

"Did you do this?" he asked as he examined it.

"Ja. I've been painting sports logos on a few." She looked at where her farm stand had been. "There were several on the shelves, but they're kindling now."

"At least you have a start on new merchandise for your shop."

She shook her head. "This isn't for the shop. It's for you. I remember you saying how much you like the Red Sox."

"Danki, Sarah Beth. How much . . . ?"

"It's a gift."

He shook his head. "You put a lot of time into this. I can't accept it."

"Why not?"

"Because . . ." He stumbled over the word twice more before he clamped his lips closed. There must be a *gut* reason why he shouldn't let her give him something she'd spent hours painting. He couldn't think of a single one that wouldn't hurt her feelings.

"Please take it, Elias." She gave him a cheeky grin. "If not for yourself, put it in your shop. Someone who's coming in to get work done on a buggy might want one too! See? You'd be helping me."

"How could I say no to such logic?"

She laughed, a sound he hadn't expected to hear that morning. It was sweeter than the first song of a lark, and he knew, despite her words, the birdhouse was a gift to thank him for his willingness to help.

What she didn't realize—and he couldn't tell her—was that asking for his help made him feel like part of a family who was always there for one another. It was a precious gift she offered him, and it made him more determined to keep his shop open in Hickory Meadows.

No matter how much someone wanted him to leave.

"What a shame about your farm stand being wrecked!" Aenti Neva filled Sarah Beth's cup with hot water. "I know how much it meant to Cora to be able to sell her vegetables. I'm sure you'll devise something by the time she starts harvesting her garden."

"We're already taking steps." Sarah Beth dipped her tea bag in her cup and watched her Aenti bustle around the comfortable kitchen.

When Sarah Beth had arrived at the house, Lovina and Luann were nowhere to be seen. Aenti Neva had explained they were spending the weekend with cousins on the other side of the family. Sarah Beth didn't want to think that her Aenti had arranged for them to be away, but she couldn't silence her dismay.

It came back triple when Aenti Neva sat at the table and said, "That's *gut* for you and Cora, but I'm glad we've got time to talk, just the two of us. Your Onkel and I think it's best for Lovina and Luann to stay here and not be disrupted when they're so near graduating from school."

"They won't graduate for two more years!"

"Sarah Beth, you must see this is the best solution for your sisters." She smiled with gentle compassion, but her eyes were calculating as she waited for a response. "You must think about what they need, not what you want."

Sarah Beth hated that expression because it was an unspoken reminder of how Aenti Neva and Onkel Bert could provide a *gut* life for the twins with no struggle. The acreage and the buildings on her family's farm were valuable, but only if she sold all of it would she have the cash she needed to provide for the twins. Three of the cows had gone dry during the past week, and though they could be bred to have calves, it would be nine months before they gave milk again. That left only nine cows, which would mean their milk sales would be down by 25 percent. In the meantime, less than fifty dollars was stored in the smallest kitchen canister.

Lord, help me decide what to do so my family can be together once more, Sarah Beth prayed silently.

Sarah Beth tried to pretend nothing was wrong when Edith visited the next day. They worked for a couple of hours on their quilt, cutting the scraps to the right sizes for more sections of the Double Wedding Ring pattern and stacking the pieces on the sewing machine in the living room. It would be brighter than the usual pastel design, which made it perfect for Edith's hope chest. Her friend adored vibrant shades and planned to use them in her new house for rag rugs and quilts.

It wasn't easy for Sarah Beth to keep her mind on the conversation between Edith and Cora, because Aenti Neva's cool words kept repeating in her head. Was it better for the twins to stay where they were for two additional years?

No! They belonged on the farm with her and Cora and Toby.

She wished she had someone to talk to about the problem, someone who could give her advice on how to deal with her Aenti and Onkel. Her thoughts answered: *Why not Elias?*

Why not? He'd seen how happy she'd been when Luann and

Lovina came to stay overnight, and he seemed to appreciate the importance of family.

Odd, though . . . he never spoke of his own family. Or was it that she hadn't bothered to ask, concentrating only on her problems? More dismay flooded her. She needed to be a better friend.

The moment she thought that, she realized that friendship might not be what she wanted to share with him. The time was wrong to consider a different relationship, but her heart was whispering how it had felt so right to be in his arms while he comforted her in the wake of the farm stand's destruction.

Her musings were interrupted when Edith asked about the combination of yellow scraps and blue ones. Sarah Beth focused on the task at hand, glad to escape from her uneasy thoughts during lunch and as they got ready for their regular shopping trip to Yoder's Store.

Cora decided to come along. She enjoyed looking around the store while Sarah Beth did her shopping, and she hinted that it was the perfect day for an ice-cream treat. Cora always ordered strawberry, and Edith's favorite was chocolate. Sarah Beth had butter pecan whenever it was available, which was about half the time. Otherwise, she chose mint chocolate chip.

A hitching pole was set in the side parking lot beyond the store. There were also parking spaces for cars. Vans driven by Englischers brought customers who lived too far away to come by buggy. As well, some plain communities in the area allowed their members to drive cars. Tourists liked to stop in to shop and gawk at the general store.

The store was the centerpiece of Hickory Meadows, though the sign over the front porch was so weathered it was impossible to read the words *Yoder's Store*. The sign wasn't necessary. If you came to the Hickory Meadows crossroads, you did your shopping at Yoder's or across the street at Mickelson's Feed and Hardware.

Sarah Beth enjoyed going into the feed store because she liked the grainy smell of animal feed and the rows of paint cans that could be mixed to any possible hue. Bins held nails and screws and more building supplies to use with the lumber sold at the rear of the store. On shelves were a selection of boots and flashlights and every other possible item not carried at Yoder's.

Today, her *gut* spirits were as flat as a board. She'd smiled at Edith's jests in the buggy and had managed to laugh, resolved to maintain the illusion everything was fine. She didn't want her friend—or her brother and sister—upset by Aenti Neva's declaration that the twins should stay in Ronks.

Abe Yoder was one of the ministers in their district. If she could get a moment alone to talk with him at his store, Sarah Beth decided she should ask him for his advice while she had the chance. She hadn't before because she didn't want to hear him say that her sisters were better off in Ronks, but she couldn't delay any longer. Her steps were lighter as she got out of the buggy. Cora was chattering like an excited squirrel, as she did every time they came to the crossroads. Edith hooked her arm through Cora's while they walked around to the front entry.

The building and front door needed painting almost as much as the sign. Bare wood could be seen through the chips of white paint, and it'd been weathered to a deep gray. The wooden porch had no hints of any color after decades of feet crossing it.

Going inside was like stepping back in time. Unlike the big-box stores on the highway to the north, Yoder's Store could have been plucked from the early twentieth century. Old-fashioned barrels on either side of the door held candy and dried fruit. Open shelving ran along the walls with goods stacked wherever they fit. Lower shelves in the center of the room on either side of the woodstove had space for more cans and bottles as well as boots and a few pairs of shoes. Two upright freezers held frozen food, while a chest freezer contained the ice cream that was served in bowls or on cones. Flour, sugar, and two types of rice were sold in bulk from the bins under the counter where a modern cash register sat next to the store's recent addition: a credit card machine. Mahlon had convinced his Daed to have one because tourists preferred to pay with a card.

"What first?" Sarah Beth asked. She noticed four or five other customers in the store; once they left and before someone else arrived, she'd discover if Abe was around and had time to talk.

"I'm going to see if there's new fabric available." Edith smiled. "I always get a *gut* deal on the remainders of the old fabric styles when the new bolts come in."

As her friend scurried away to the left corner of the store, Sarah Beth got a cart and led Cora to the nearest shelves to begin their shopping. They needed store-bought vegetables because the last of beans and peas she and Cora had canned last fall had all been eaten. She was glad her sister had planted two more rows of each this year, especially if the twins came home.

Not if. When!

"Want to look at the ice cream," Cora announced.

"Go ahead, but don't order any until I have a chance to select what I want."

With a nod, her sister excitedly rushed to the ice-cream freezer.

Sarah Beth glanced around but didn't see Abe. If she didn't have the chance to talk to him today, she'd speak with him on the next church Sunday. In the meantime, she'd see if Elias had any advice for her.

"Ah, here you are!" said a deep voice, shocking her so much she almost dropped a can of peas.

"Mahlon, you scared me." She noticed a small cut on his forehead. It was almost healed. "How did you hurt yourself?"

"The usual." He tapped the shelf, and she recalled how he'd banged his head on one when he first started working in the store.

"You need to be more careful."

"Tell me about it!" He smiled, his eyes raking her as if she were for sale. "Sorry I startled you. I didn't mean to, but you were concentrating on the can."

"Just thinking." She kept the can between her and him, wishing he'd stop staring at her. Since he'd started flirting with her after Sunday services, she'd grown less comfortable in his company. She was grateful for the other customers so she wasn't alone with him.

"Deep thoughts?" he asked.

"No. Deciding whether to get cans of corn along with other vegetables."

"Planning on having company?"

She frowned. He was acting strange, and she wished he'd stop. "No more than usual."

"Your new neighbor?"

"What's wrong?" she asked, too unnerved to reply.

"Keep an eye on him, Sarah Beth." Mahlon dropped his voice. It was so quiet she had to strain to hear each word as he leaned one elbow on the top of the shelving unit. "You know my Daed talks to other ministers and ordained men."

"I can see why he'd do that." *But I can't see why you're telling me this or warning me about Elias.*

As if she'd said it out loud, he whispered, "So trust me when I say what I'm telling you is the truth. The people in the town where Elias used to live were glad to see him go because he used to set fires."

"What?" The single word squeaked from her. "Elias Stutzman?"

He nodded.

"Are you sure?"

He nodded again. "When he was a teenager. It was mischief until a fire he caused burned a barn almost twelve years ago."

She didn't want to believe what he was saying, but she could tell Mahlon was sincere. "Was anyone hurt?"

"No." He spoke the word almost reluctantly. "It was a storage barn where they kept hay."

"How did they know it was him?"

Mahlon shrugged. "I'm not a policeman, and Daed doesn't tell me everything." His tone suggested it would be better if Abe did share with his son what was discussed by the district's leaders. "Elias Stutzman was arrested."

Sarah Beth stared at the pitted shelf that had lost every hint of varnish. The intensity in Mahlon's eyes unsettled her as much as his words. Could what he said be true?

Elias seldom spoke of his past. He never mentioned his youth or his family. Was this the secret he was keeping?

"I know this is hard for you to hear," Mahlon went on. "But I thought you should know because he's your neighbor and your brother is spending a lot of time at his place."

"Are you sure Abe was talking about the same man?"

"Ja. I wouldn't have said anything if I'd had any doubts that the Elias Stutzman living across the creek from you is the one who was arrested."

Sarah Beth put the can into the cart before her numb fingers dropped it. Elias? Arrested? She didn't want to believe what Mahlon said, but if he'd heard the story from his Daed . . .

Toby!

She gripped the side of the cart. She'd agreed to let Toby work for Elias in part because she wanted a *gut* male role model for her brother. She couldn't have been more mistaken. How was she going to keep Toby from going to Elias's shop? Her brother had become very responsible about taking care of the barn work and his other tasks since she'd insisted he finish them before going across the covered bridge. He'd be furious if she changed the conditions of their deal, and he'd be right. Only if she explained the truth would he understand . . . maybe.

She couldn't spread a story that might not be true. Mahlon must have wanted to be as careful because he'd spoken in a whisper. Yet she couldn't let her brother spend time with a man who'd been arrested . . . and kept the truth from her. Letting her family become more involved with him would give her Aenti another reason to keep the twins from coming home.

Her heart threatened to break into dozens of tiny pieces at the thought of pushing Elias from her life, but she couldn't take the chance. Not when reuniting her family was at stake.

"Listen to me, Sarah Beth." Mahlon leaned toward her again. "I don't want to see you or anyone in your family get hurt."

"Neither do I."

"Watch yourself around your new neighbor."

Elias appraised the wheel he'd put on Abe Yoder's buggy. It wasn't level. Running his fingers along it, he sighed when he felt a small bump he'd missed while the wheel was off. He'd thought he'd checked every inch of it, but he hadn't caught the invisible blemish.

"Toby?" he called, and then he remembered the boy wasn't coming over until later.

With a wordless grumble, Elias reached for his wrench and began to loosen the bolts holding the wheel in place. He made sure the blocks supporting the buggy were solid before he yanked the wheel off, almost knocking himself on his rear end. The wheel clanged against the floor, but he kept it from rolling away by hooking a foot in it.

He almost cheered when he heard the door open. "Toby, get back here! I could use your help!"

"I'm not Toby," called Sarah Beth.

What was she doing here at this hour? Not that he was complaining. Any chance to see her was a blessing he wouldn't question.

Standing, he started to smile, but she regarded him with a somber expression. She locked her fingers together in front of her, a motion he'd come to realize meant she was upset.

"Elias, I wanted to let you know Toby won't be coming today," she said without a hint of emotion in her voice.

"Danki. Tomorrow—"

"He won't be coming tomorrow either."

His brows lowered. "Or the day after that?"

Instead of giving him a direct answer, she said, "He's my brother, Elias, and I'm responsible for him. He has obligations to our family and needs to do them instead of going off on a lark."

"I don't consider his working here a lark, and he doesn't either."

"Like I said, he's my responsibility. I'm the one who makes these decisions for him." Without another word, she opened the door and left.

Elias tossed his wrench onto his worktable. It clattered against the other tools he'd left there, but for once he didn't check to make sure they hadn't been damaged.

She'd heard.

He wasn't sure how or who'd told her about the fire that changed his life. His senses were filled with the dank smell of water-soaked beams charred and fallen to the ground. The odor was only in his memory, but it stank and was as real as the day he'd watched the barn burn to the ground. As the firefighters doused the fire, he'd had no idea what lay ahead for him.

Arrest and questioning and shame.

Sarah Beth knew he'd messed up his life. He couldn't imagine any other reason for her to become chillier to him than she'd been the first time she'd come looking for her brother.

He couldn't blame her. He was the last person she'd want her brother to learn from, because she had no idea what he might teach Toby in addition to repairing buggies.

He'd thought he'd left that part of his past behind him, but it'd caught up with him and ended any chance he had to relish being part of a family. Even more painful was knowing he'd never hold Sarah Beth again.

10

Sarah Beth climbed down the wooden ladder she'd propped against her shop's front wall. When she reached the ground, she smiled. The sign she'd taken care to paint now hung over the building's front door: *King's Kountry Krafts*.

The letters appeared to be growing out of tufts of grass and wildflowers. The design matched the one she'd put on her latest batch of birdhouses. It was a bit fancy, but it would catch the eyes of tourists driving by once she put a similar sign at the end of the farm lane. That sign was ready for Toby to set in place. Unlike the one on the shop, it was made from combining three slats. One had the name of the shop. The next one listed the items they had for sale and would be changed with the unfolding of the seasons and what was harvested in the garden. The lowest one had the obligatory *Closed on Sundays* sign that hung in front of all Amish businesses.

Setting the ladder on the ground, Sarah Beth wiped her hands and swept dust and bits of wood off her apron. No matter how much she and Cora and Edith scrubbed the shop, there always seemed to be places they missed. In this case, it'd been the simple lintel atop the front door.

The interior of the shop would require another two weeks of work to get the shelving in place and stock it with her birdhouses and Edith's quillows and small quilt hangings. One of her neighbors had asked about selling the faceless rag dolls tourists loved to buy as souvenirs, and another was interested in having Sarah Beth display her quilted pot holders and tea cozies. Sarah Beth was going to have to find a few more tables so she could show off Cora's fresh vegetables as well as the chowchow, pickled onions, and jams she and her sister made each fall.

It would have been much simpler if Elias had helped as he'd offered. She'd put Toby to work instead. He'd protested until she told him she needed his help badly. Guilt tormented her. She should have been honest with him about everything, including what Mahlon had shared, but she hadn't wanted to deal with Toby's disappointment while trying to handle her own.

She'd find a way to tell Toby, but not until the shop was open and the twins were home for good.

That was what was important. Her brother and Cora were as eager to have Luann and Lovina home as she was, which was, she suspected, the reason Toby had acquiesced to working for her instead of going to the buggy shop.

Focus on the business!

Looking around again, she walked to the counter that wasn't much more than a slab of wood they'd found in the barn and set up on wooden legs. She wondered how long it would take her to earn enough money to buy a used cash register. For now, she planned to use a money box and a calculator. She wasn't ready to take credit cards as Yoder's Store did, so she made sure she had a lockable money box.

She sighed. Before her farm stand was run over and the vandalism at Elias's buggy shop, she'd left an honesty box out by the road. Those who stopped by and bought something could put their money in the box and take any change due them. She wasn't sure if she should do that again. That her faith in the goodness of others had been strained bothered her deeply.

Glancing at the wires attached to the big barn, Sarah Beth was glad her shop had plenty of windows. She didn't want her customers stumbling around in the dark. Once she had a cash register installed, she'd need to have the building hooked to the electric lines. Until then, King's Kountry Krafts would be open only during the day.

As she closed the door behind her, she heard a familiar rattle. Her heart jumped in her chest at the thought that it might be Elias coming over the bridge and up the road. She silenced her rebellious excitement. Nothing had changed . . . including her heart.

The buggy turned into her lane. It wasn't Elias's because a black horse was pulling it. Who could it be?

When the driver called a greeting, Sarah Beth was astonished. Why was Mahlon coming to the farm? Other than for a church Sunday, she couldn't recall him ever setting foot on the property.

She was more surprised when she realized he wasn't alone. A woman sat to his left in the buggy. Sarah Beth didn't recognize the woman, who was taller than Mahlon and looked reed-thin next to his broad shoulders. Her bright red hair was neat beneath her Kapp, and her dark green cape dress offered the perfect foil for her eyes of the same color. Like Sarah Beth, she wore a black apron around her waist, and dark stockings and sneakers.

Mahlon had on his regular light blue shirt beneath his black suspenders. Sarah noticed that his straw hat sat at a jaunty angle that wouldn't have been approved by their bishop. The heels of his heavy work boots struck the stones in the driveway.

He called another greeting as he and the woman walked over to Sarah Beth. As she rested the ladder on its side against the base of the shop's wall, she asked, "Are you enjoying this pretty day?"

"We are." He grinned as if she'd said something funny, and his eyes sparkled when he turned to the woman with him. "Sarah Beth, this is Vera Swartzentruber. She lives near Gap. Her Daed is a deacon there."

"It's nice to meet you, Vera."

She gave Sarah Beth a half smile but said nothing. Was she shy? If so, it was important to make her feel comfortable.

"Do you have time," Sarah Beth asked, "to enjoy some ice tea? The porch swing is nice at this time of day because the sun is to your back. We can sit and talk."

Mahlon nodded. "*Gut*, because I've got something I want to talk to you about."

"What?"

"I'm interested in buying your farm."

Sarah Beth stared at him in disbelief. She must have heard him wrong.

Mahlon Yoder wanted to buy the farm? He'd never worked on a farm because he'd grown up at the family store. In fact, he used to tease the other Kinder about having dirt beneath their fingernails and stains on their clothing.

"That's a surprise," she replied when she realized she must say something.

"Why? Isn't it every plain man's hope to spend his life tending to God's greatest gift to mankind? The very earth itself." His smile broadened as if he wanted to include Vera and her in his plans.

Sarah Beth tried to ignore the quiver of distaste rippling through her as she thought of how Mahlon had flirted with her. He'd made her nervous then, and his expression made her as ill at ease now.

"You've always talked about the day when you'll be in charge of Yoder's Store." She wanted to believe what he was saying, but Mahlon Yoder was the last man she would have guessed harbored a secret wish to take on the hard life of a farmer.

"I've decided I like fresh air better than being stuck in a store." He stared at the house. "How many bedrooms?"

"Five plus one in the Dawdi Haus, but we haven't used the Dawdi Haus in years except for storage."

"Bathrooms?"

"One on the first floor of the main house and another in the Dawdi Haus." She chided herself for acceding to his assumption she'd be eager to sell him her family's farm.

"Toby milks a dozen cows, ain't so?"

"Mahlon, I haven't said I'm interested in selling the farm."

He acted as if he hadn't heard her. Walking toward the main barn with Vera, he paused to look at the chicken coop and the small barn where the diesel engine provided the compressed air that powered the milking lines and kept the milk in the dairy storage tank chilled.

Sarah Beth trailed them, not sure how to stop the impromptu tour. When she noticed Cora peeking past the kitchen door, she decided to put a halt to this. Cora would be distraught at the idea of selling the farm.

"Mahlon!" she called.

When he didn't respond, she planted herself between him and the main barn. He started to edge around her, but she grabbed his sleeve. She wasn't sure if he was startled by her action or by her frown. Either way, he stopped.

"What is it?" he asked in a tone that suggested *she* was the one trespassing.

"I never said I wanted to sell the farm."

"Everyone knows you want to get your little sisters home, and I don't have to tell you two extra mouths are going to be pricey. I figured you'd appreciate an offer on the farm so you can take care of them."

Sarah Beth lifted her fingers off his sleeve. He hadn't said anything she hadn't considered, but she'd spoken to nobody about selling the farm, not even Toby. Had others come to the same conclusion as Mahlon? Was she risking the family reunion she craved by holding onto the farm?

"It's a nice farm." Vera's voice was wispy, as if she had to take a breath between each syllable. "I don't think I'd mind living here."

"We've been happy here," Sarah Beth quickly said, even more unsettled by Vera's unexpected comment.

"All *gut* things come to an end, ain't so?" Mahlon's smile was kind, but she saw calculation in his eyes. Like the storekeeper he was, he was trying to gauge how much her family's farm was worth. "That's all right when the ends are justified."

"You're assuming too much, Mahlon." Sarah Beth regarded him until he looked away, his easy smile fading. "I haven't made plans to sell the farm."

"I'll give you a fair price for it." He spoke a number that astounded her. Land prices had risen in Lancaster County, but she hadn't expected the farm to be worth so much. With that sum, she could buy a small house and have room for her whole family. "What do you say, Sarah Beth?"

"I need to think about it."

"Don't think too long. I might find a farm that suits me better."

Sarah Beth nodded but didn't reply. Why would Mahlon think she'd agree to any offer—even a generous one—without discussing it with her family?

"What's that building?" asked Vera. "King's Kountry Krafts? Is it a shop? Mahlon mentioned you sold birdhouses at your farm stand." She glanced around. "I didn't see it when we drove in."

"We don't use it any longer." She didn't want to complicate this already-complicated conversation with an explanation of what had happened to the farm stand.

"So you're opening a shop?"

"How about I get a jug of ice tea for us?" Sarah Beth said instead of answering Vera. She found the other woman's abrupt intensity disconcerting.

No doubt Vera was trying to prove to Mahlon she didn't mind he'd stopped in at the farm while he was taking her for a drive.

This time Mahlon accepted the invitation for a refreshing drink. As they walked toward the front porch, Sarah Beth asked about his family and asked Vera what she thought of southern Lancaster County. She received terse answers, but she didn't let that sway her from preventing them from returning to the topic of her selling the farm.

As they walked onto the porch, Vera asked, "Aren't we close to where Elias Stutzman lives?"

Sarah Beth looked away so the other woman couldn't see her reaction. Vera's question had come out of nowhere, but her studied tone suggested it wasn't a casual inquiry.

When Sarah Beth didn't answer, Mahlon did. "I think he lives somewhere around here. Sarah Beth?"

She couldn't avoid responding to his direct question. As if their curiosity didn't unsettle her, she replied, "I assumed you knew, Mahlon, that his shop is on the far side of the covered bridge."

"Why?"

"He's working on a buggy for your Daed."

"Is that where the old buggy went?" Mahlon gave a short laugh. "I didn't know."

"Do you need work done on a buggy?"

"No no," Vera answered and smiled. "I heard someone mention his name at Mahlon's Daed's store."

"Do you know Elias?" She reached to open the front door.

"It's more that I know *of* him rather than actually knowing him."

Sarah Beth froze with her hand on the doorknob. Was Vera referring to the story Mahlon had told when Sarah Beth last saw him? She couldn't guess what else it might be.

Lifting her hand off the knob, she looked at the two behind her. "What do you . . . ?"

Mahlon cut her off as he said, "We need to go. Think about my offer. I don't know how long it'll be *gut*. We need to go."

Startled by Mahlon's abrupt announcement, Sarah Beth started to ask a question. He ignored her and steered Vera toward his buggy. They got in, and he slapped the reins as if on his way to fight a fire.

The buggy raced at an unsafe speed away from the house. When it didn't slow as it made the turn onto the road, she held her breath. She could see the wheels strain to remain on the ground.

Why had they left so suddenly? She'd been sure Mahlon had intended to push her for an answer to his offer, but he'd left without an explanation. What was going on?

Elias stared at the buggy speeding toward him as he was about to walk up the lane to Sarah Beth's house. He jumped aside into the high grass in the ditch along the road. Fighting for his balance, he grabbed the mailbox so he didn't fall into the water at the bottom of the ditch.

The buggy rushed past him so fast he felt a breeze in his flushed face. Nobody should be driving so recklessly.

When he caught sight of the occupants, thoughts of the driver endangering himself, his passenger, and his horse fled his mind. He wanted to deny what his eyes were showing him, but as he turned to watch the buggy vanish over a rise in the road, he knew he wasn't mistaken about the tall woman with the bright red hair.

Vera Swartzentruber.

There couldn't be another woman with her height and coloring among the plain folk in the county. She lived north of Hickory Meadows, near the small town of Gap. What was she doing at Sarah Beth's house? With Mahlon Yoder, if Elias wasn't mistaken—and he didn't think he was.

His hope that he'd left his past behind when he came to Hickory Meadows vanished. It'd found him.

Or had it?

Vera was the sister of his onetime best friend and fellow troublemaker, Roy Swartzentruber. Could there be a legitimate reason why she was at Sarah Beth's house?

Jumping onto the road, Elias strode up the lane. He wouldn't get to the truth by standing in a ditch. He needed to ask Sarah Beth. He winced as he realized he might have to admit to the tales of his past mistakes.

Sarah Beth was toting a ladder through the door of the small building she was making into a shop. She halted when she saw him approaching. Putting the ladder down, she said, "I didn't expect to see you today."

In spite of the cold words they'd spoken the last time he'd seen her, his breath was swept away by how the sunlight glistened off her blonde hair, turning it into spun gold. As he closed the distance between them, he saw the unmistakable signs of tension on her face. Her lips were compressed, ruining her attempt to smile. Lines he'd never noticed creased her forehead, and her eyes darted about, avoiding his.

What was she trying to hide? Was she bothered by him appearing unannounced after she'd severed the faint ties between him and her family?

Or—and he gritted his teeth at the thought—had Vera done or said something to upset her? Something about him and what happened before he left their district?

"I hope I'm not interrupting your work." What a stupid remark! Of course he was interrupting her. "I was walking past, and I thought I'd stop and see how you were getting along with the shop."

If she had any suspicions he was avoiding the truth, she didn't mention it. Instead she said, "I just hung the sign. Does it look straight to you?"

He glanced at it, though questions were burning on his lips. "Ja, it looks fine to me."

"If you're here to talk about Toby, I can tell you I'll need his help for another week."

"I understand." Before he could halt himself, he blurted, "That wasn't Vera Swartzentruber, was it?"

"It was." Her brows lowered in a frown. "She said she knows you, so you must know her, ain't so?"

It was a loaded question and one that could explode in his face, ruining the last chance of saving their friendship. But he didn't want to be only Sarah Beth's friend. Friendship seemed too tepid an emotion to describe the sensations sweeping over him whenever he saw her or was near to her . . . or thought of her.

He resisted the temptation to tell Sarah Beth everything he knew about Vera and her brother Roy. To explain about the Swartzentrubers would mean having to tell her everything about himself.

He wasn't ready to risk that. Not when he might be able to bridge the chasm between them.

"Ja, I know her. We went to the same school."

How could he explain the trouble he and Roy had gotten into? Trouble that kept escalating until the horrible fire that had scared Elias straight. It hadn't done the same for Roy, but Roy never seemed to be blamed for anything because Roy's Daed was the deacon, the person who punished Elias for the pranks both boys had devised.

"What was Vera doing here?" he asked.

"She came with Mahlon." Her gaze slid away from his.

He sighed. She wasn't going to tell him more. Any connection there might have been between them was gone, stolen by the stories of the mistakes he'd made. He might as well have been a stranger standing there.

If he said something before he turned to leave—or if she did—the words disappeared as he strode away. He'd been a fool to trust her as much as he had. Every person he'd believed was on his side had turned their backs on him.

This time, for what might be the first time in his life, he hadn't given someone the cause to do so. He didn't need to because a man couldn't alter his past even if he changed his heart.

Yet he'd thought Sarah Beth would be different . . .

He'd been wrong.

11

To say Elias was shocked when Toby walked into his buggy shop two days later was a gross understatement. The boy hadn't come since Sarah Beth put him to work fixing her shop.

Another pang cut through Elias. He'd looked forward to working on Sarah Beth's shop, helping her as she'd helped him and spending time with her. He'd avoided driving past the Kings' farm. Yesterday he'd gone more than two miles out of his way so there was no chance he'd encounter her.

He was being ridiculous, and he was miserable. Not going toward the Kings' farm lane didn't ease his misery. Nothing did. He couldn't lose himself in work, which had always been his haven.

"You shouldn't be here." Elias hated the dull tone of his voice, but he was trying to feel nothing. He'd give up feeling happy later if he could stop feeling bad now.

"I know." Toby shuffled his feet against the floor.

The boy scanned the space, and Elias saw hunger in his eyes. Toby wanted to return to working with him. Sarah Beth's brother showed a true talent for handling tools as well as diagnosing a problem and devising a way to fix it.

"So why are you here?"

"I'll be graduating on Friday, y'know."

"I think you may have mentioned that once or twice." He shot a grin at the boy, and then his brows lowered as he saw that Toby was as uneasy as someone who'd been called to the deacon's house to explain a misdeed.

He knew too well how that felt.

Forget the past! How many times did he have to repeat those words before his brain would listen? More than he already had, because his memory of the fire and the aftermath stuck with him like a burr on a wool sock.

"What's wrong, Toby?" he asked.

"Nothing." He shuffled his feet. "You're not from around here, so you don't know."

"Know what?"

"We always have a picnic before our graduation ceremony."

"A *gut* idea. Let everyone have a chance to celebrate."

Toby nodded. "We can bring our families. I want you to come. Will you?"

Elias's first instinct was to say that he'd be there, because he wanted to be counted as part of someone's family. Caution halted him. "Does your sister know you're inviting me?"

"Sure," the boy said, but his gaze slid away.

He'd learned the game the boy thought he couldn't figure out. He'd played the same one as a teenager. Give an adult an honest answer to a question, but don't share everything you know.

As if it were unimportant, Elias asked, "So Sarah Beth knows you're inviting me?"

"Oh, you meant *that* sister." Toby laughed, the sound falling flat.

"You haven't answered my question. Does Sarah Beth know you're inviting me?"

"Not exactly."

Which Elias translated as meaning the boy hadn't mentioned his plan to her. "Don't you think you should mention that you're inviting me so she's not surprised when I show up?"

"Everyone will be there." A stubborn frown settled on his volatile face. "We're supposed to bring our families and our friends. Aren't we friends?"

Elias faced Toby. "As your friend I'm suggesting that graduation wouldn't be the best time to surprise your sister."

Toby mulled that over. "So you want Sarah Beth to know I asked you."

"Ja."

"Okay." Without another word, Toby left.

Elias sighed and returned to the task of reinstalling the dash in the buggy. He hoped Toby could persuade Sarah Beth to agree to let Elias attend the graduation. It would be an illusion, but for a few hours he could again feel as if he were part of a family.

Caught up in his work, it seemed a short time later when he heard footsteps coming toward the shop. Elias looked at the wall clock and was astonished that hours had elapsed while he'd contorted his long form inside the buggy to attach a screw in one place and a bolt in another.

He untangled himself from the narrow space between the seat and the front of the buggy as the door opened. Expecting it was Abe Yoder coming to check on the progress of his vehicle, he rubbed his aching left shoulder. It'd been propping him on the floor for the last hour.

That discomfort was forgotten when Sarah Beth walked in. She looked as anxious as she had the first time she'd come to the shop. It was as if the past weeks had never happened.

"Toby said you wanted to see me," she said.

Elias gave a terse laugh. "It'd be more honest to say that he didn't want to be the one to tell you what he's got planned." Raising his hands, he added, "It's not about coming to work here. He knows you need him for your shop."

"That's *gut.*" She relaxed.

"Toby asked me to his graduation and the picnic before it. I told him you must be okay with it."

Her shoulders eased a bit more from their jittery tension, and a faint smile softened her face. "I'm glad Toby asked you."

"You are?"

"Ja. We're neighbors, Elias, and being at odds isn't easy."

He should tell her sweeping the past under a rug and pretending it'd never happened wasn't the best way to rebuild trust. He should be honest with her and ask that she be the same with him.

Instead he said, "I agree."

"So you'll come to Toby's graduation?"

"I wouldn't miss it for the world." It felt *gut* to speak the truth.

The small, light brown schoolhouse was set on one corner of a crossroads about a mile from the Kings' farm. A split rail fence divided it from the field and a large white barn. Four swings were in use near the ball field where the students were already choosing sides for the game they'd play before the graduation ceremony. On the other side of the school, set beneath the shade of a pair of trees, was the two-door outhouse for use by the scholars.

More than a dozen buggies were parked along the dirt road that edged a meandering creek. When Elias reined in his horse, a lad came rushing forward as if they were having a wedding. As he would have done for the guests of the bride and groom, he unhitched Wonder Boy, marked a number on his harness with chalk, and wrote the same number on the side of Elias's buggy. The boy grinned as he walked Wonder Boy toward the meadow across the road from the school. The horse whinnied to the others already there.

Elias turned to walk toward the school, unsure of where he was supposed to go or what he was supposed to do. Several people called a greeting in his direction and others waved. He recognized them from Sunday services. Glancing around, he saw no sign of Vera or Mahlon.

Why was he worrying about *them*? He was here to celebrate an important day in Toby's life, the day when he went from being a scholar to being an adult member of the community. It should be the first of many vital days ahead for the lad as he began attending youth events and found a girl to walk out with before he was baptized and became a full member of the Leit.

Elias smiled when he heard familiar voices. Sarah Beth's twin sisters were shrieking with laughter as they played tag with the other Kinder.

A hand clapped his arm. "You came!" Toby was as excited as the twins.

Elias's gaze was caught by Sarah Beth's. He looked at her as he answered the boy. His words were intended for her as much as her brother. "I told you I would, and one thing I've always been is a man of my word."

Others might accuse Elias of Hochmut for the pride in his voice as he spoke those simple words, but Sarah Beth guessed they meant a lot to him. The wall she'd tried to raise around her heart shifted again. She'd been wrong to let Mahlon's stories prejudice her against Elias. "Judge not, that ye be not judged." The verse from Matthew warned that looking into someone's soul and passing judgment on it was solely God's responsibility. She needed to remember that.

She wanted to believe that she would have come to the conclusion much sooner if she hadn't been so taken aback by Mahlon's offer to buy her farm. Every thought since then had been consumed by wondering if she were delaying the inevitable by hesitating. Should she accept his offer and start looking for a new home for her family? Toby didn't want to be a farmer, but to put a price on what had been in her family for many generations . . . She wasn't ready to do that, but she had to face the truth that if she waited, she might have to sell the farm for less.

"We're glad you're here, Elias," she said when she realized the silence had gone on too long.

"I've never been to a graduation picnic." He glanced at the school's front porch where baskets were lined up. "Was I supposed to bring something?"

"You're *my* guest," Toby said. "You don't need to bring anything. We'll have more than we can eat anyhow."

"That's true." Sarah Beth laughed, her first honest laugh since Mahlon had whispered the unsavory rumors about Elias.

No! She wasn't going to think about the past. Today was about the future.

Sarah Beth stepped aside as Cora pushed between her and Elias. Her sister was quivering with strong emotions. When Sarah Beth put consoling hands on her sister's shoulders, Cora shrugged them off.

"You're too old for me, Elias Stutzman." Cora folded her arms and raised her chin. "I've got a new boyfriend. You need to get yourself a new girlfriend."

Elias affixed a sad smile on his face, but relief glowed in his eyes. "If that's what you want, Cora, I won't stand in your way. If your new boyfriend doesn't treat you nice, you let me know. Okay?"

"Okay. I want ice cream." She walked toward the school to get in line where two women were scooping freshly churned ice cream from a tub.

Toby ran after her, joining the line, which was growing longer as the Kinder realized the treat was ready.

"Well, I've been dumped." Elias chuckled. "It's nice, I've got to say, to be told the truth without someone beating around the bush."

"That's Cora for you. She gets right to the point."

"I'd like it if everyone did."

She smiled and shook her head. "I used to think that, but I never know what she'll say next. Danki for being nice and playing along with Cora."

"My pleasure. She's a sweet girl, and I enjoyed being her beau." He laughed again. "Most of the time. Shall we get some ice cream too?"

"A wunderbar idea."

As Sarah Beth walked with him toward where bowls of strawberry ice cream were being served as fast as the women could scoop it, she was aware of furtive glances in their direction. She tried to ignore the looks filled with curiosity about why she was with him.

It wasn't difficult to do until Cora proved she'd meant what she'd said to Elias when she told him to get a new girlfriend. Her attempts at matchmaking would have been funny if they hadn't been so public.

She bumped into Sarah Beth, knocking the plastic spoon from her hand. "Oh, you don't need another one," Cora said. "There aren't any extras, and you can share Elias's."

"I've had enough anyhow." Sarah Beth started toward the barrel where the trash was being collected.

"You can't waste ice cream." Cora jabbed a finger at Elias. "Tell her not to waste ice cream."

Laughter wove through his voice. "You heard your sister, Sarah Beth. You shouldn't waste ice cream." Holding out his spoon, he said, "I'm done, if you want to rinse this off and use it."

Cora walked away, dismayed that the result of her machinations wasn't what she'd hoped. She didn't give up, though. She sent Luann to tell Sarah Beth and Elias to sit together on a blanket set off to one side while they were served slices of cake and more ice cream.

"You'll need to share a spoon *now*," Cora said with a rare assertiveness.

When she discovered that Toby had brought an extra spoon when he joined Elias and his sister, she was annoyed. Not only at him for offering the other spoon, but because he'd intruded on what Cora saw as an opportunity for Elias to make Sarah Beth his new girlfriend.

When she realized how the other families were beginning to notice Cora's matchmaking, Sarah Beth took her sister aside and explained how Cora had had the chance to find a boyfriend, who was the older brother of one of the graduating scholars. As he was so focused on his apprenticeship at his Daed's small engine shop, Sarah Beth doubted he had any idea Cora believed he was her boyfriend.

"You chose your new love, Cora," she said. "You must let Elias do the same."

"He needs a girlfriend and you need a boyfriend. You're old, so anyone can see you need help. I want to help you."

Sarah Beth wasn't sure whether to be insulted by her sister's blunt words or to laugh. She didn't do either as she repeated that matchmaking wasn't appropriate on Toby's special day.

She seemed to convince her sister, or so Sarah Beth thought until Cora insisted that Sarah Beth sit next to Elias when they went into the school for the graduation exercises. Again Cora's attempts failed because Elias gave his chair to a very pregnant woman.

The ceremony was almost identical to the one Sarah Beth had been part of a decade before. It was amazing to think that in two years, Luann and Lovina would be graduating as well.

Would it be from this school? Her sisters had been excited about coming to see Toby graduate, but they'd spent the time during the ride from Onkel Bert's house discussing how they were going to spend their summer. They talked about their friends in the school they attended and the events that would be held during the coming months. Not once had they mentioned coming home or visiting again overnight.

Lovina and Luann were growing away from the rest of their family . . . and from her. She fought to restrain her tears at the thought of losing them as she'd lost too many others. How easy it would have been to confront them with her feelings, but she held her tongue. They were twelve years old, hardly more than Kinder. She should be pleased they were happy, because they'd been grief-stricken when Grossmammi Miriam died.

Sarah Beth had never intended for her sisters to be gone so long. Why was she hesitating about selling the farm? It was dirt and rocks and buildings. She'd lose her new shop before it opened, but she and Toby could build another farm stand where she'd sell her birdhouses. Yet without an actual shop, would she be able to earn enough to keep the family together?

She looked at Luann and Lovina, who were watching while the scholars sang and recited from memory. They applauded extra-loudly for the girls who'd been their best friends as well as when Toby shared the poem he'd worked for two weeks to memorize.

Sarah Beth was proud of him too, though she couldn't help noticing he spoke in a rhythm identical to the milking machine in the barn. He must have practiced while milking the cows. She thought nobody else noticed until Elias grinned and pantomimed milking by hand.

The ceremony went quickly. When it was finished, the families who'd been an enthusiastic audience congratulated the now-former scholars and the teacher before drifting outside toward their buggies. Few lingered because it was time to start evening chores.

As she waited for Cinnamon to be brought from across the road, Sarah Beth thanked Elias for coming. "It means a lot to Toby that you're here."

"It means a lot to me to be asked," he replied, and she heard the loneliness that laced through his voice too often.

Toby joined them. He seemed to be standing a bit taller, enjoying the beginning of his transition from Kind to adult. How long would it take Sarah Beth to remember not to treat him like a youngster?

After he collected hugs from his sisters, Toby shook Elias's hand with every bit of his new dignity.

"Toby," Elias said as he released Toby's hand, "if your sister can spare you, I'd like to offer you a part-time job at the shop. I can't afford a full-time helper yet, but you can continue to learn how to repair buggies."

His face could barely contain his grin. "Can I, Sarah Beth?"

She looked from her brother to Elias and was shocked to see entreaty on his face as well. Elias needed Toby's help, and she'd seen how well they got along. For the first time, she thought of Elias living and working alone day after day. No wonder she sensed his isolation.

"Elias, I'd like to talk to you alone before I say ja or no."

When Toby started to protest that he wasn't a kid any longer, Elias said, "Your sister cares about your well-being. Not just yours, but your whole family's." He grinned. "Don't worry. I can be persuasive."

Toby nodded but couldn't hide his anxiety. Being able to continue working with Elias was vitally important to him.

Sarah Beth and Elias walked around the side of the school so the building was between them and her siblings. A picnic table overlooked the ball field that was in use every school day when there wasn't too much snow.

Sitting, Sarah Beth said, "I need to clear the air between us before I give Toby permission to work with you."

"All right." His shoulders rose as if he were about to lift the schoolhouse.

"First, I want to say you're helping my brother in ways I never could. He'll be a better man because of you." She hated having to add, "That's true, ain't so?"

"I hope so, because I'm not the man I was." He scowled. "Or more accurately, I'm not the angry and lost boy I was. I banished that young fool from my life after I hurt those who'd given me a place to sleep and food to eat."

Sarah Beth's heart pushed aside another section of the thick wall she had raised to protect it. Elias's words told her much even as they said little. He hadn't said he'd risked hurting those he loved or those who loved him. Only the ones who'd provided him with the basics to stay alive. Nothing more.

Was that the source of his solitude and his yearning to belong? She'd perceived it in him at times—always, she realized with amazement, when she'd invited him to do something with her family.

"I've heard about a fire and you being arrested." There. She'd said the words she'd dreaded speaking, fearful of hurting him more.

"I want you to know the truth."

"I'm listening."

"It's not a pleasant story."

"I told you I'd listen, and I will."

Elias wondered if Sarah Beth knew how seldom he'd heard those words. While he was growing up, rarely had anyone listened to him—*really* listened. Instead, they'd lectured him, listing his faults and blaming him for what he'd done . . . and for what he hadn't done. He'd learned to stay quiet and accept the punishments whether he deserved them or not. As time went on he convinced himself that if he was going to suffer the consequences, he might as well do what everyone believed he had.

Sarah Beth was willing to hear him out. It was an astounding gift she was giving him, and he was grateful, more grateful than words could express.

In exchange for her kindness, he owed her the truth. All of it.

He sat beside her. "When I was a few years older than Toby, I joined a Rumspringa group called the Hooligans. I know it's a strange name for an Amish group of kids. We chose it because we wanted something as far from plain as we could get. One time when we pulled a prank, an Englischer called us a bunch of hooligans. We liked the sound, so we used it as our name." He drew in a deep breath. "In retrospect, it should have been a sign we were headed along a bad path."

He waited for her to say something, but she remained silent, as she'd said she would. He saw compassion in her eyes, and he wondered how much she already knew about his shameful past.

"Our pranks were at first pretty harmless. Leaving the phone off the hook in phone shacks so no calls could come in. Letting sheep out of a field or putting cows into a hayfield. One of the guys had a car, so we rode about and pretended we were cool, smoking until we got sick and threw up. Then the pranks got more serious. I tried to separate myself from the group, but they were my friends." He gulped hard. "And my family."

"Rumspringa gangs can feel like that," she said. "I've seen it with others, which is why I keep a close watch on Toby and remind him how much his family depends on him."

"If I'd had someone like you in my life, things might have been different. Everything came to a head when one fellow hid a portable radio and some beer in Solomon Yutzy's hayloft. We planned to go there while everyone else was at church. We did, but Solomon saw us and chased us away. Two days later his barn burned to the ground. He believed—as others did—that someone set the fire in retaliation for him running us off. The day after the fire, I realized that my cell phone was gone. I had no idea where I'd lost it. I asked my friends, but none of them had it."

She frowned. "I don't understand. What does your missing cell phone have to do with the fire?"

"Because a phone, melted into a puddle of plastic and metal, was found right at the spot they believe the fire started. It was possible the phone caused the fire, though the fire marshal said it might have begun for a different reason. I was questioned, shown the phone, and asked if it was mine. When I said it was, I was arrested."

"Even though you couldn't identify it because it was melted?" When he nodded, she asked, "If the authorities believed there wasn't proof, why were you treated as if you'd set the fire?"

"Because there wasn't any proof I didn't."

"Don't be absurd. Even if you did drop your phone in the barn, it was an accident. It's true you weren't supposed to be in the hayloft, but sneaking into a barn to listen to the radio while on Rumspringa is a whole different matter than arson."

"The police realized that too, and I was released."

She put her hand on his arm in gentle compassion. "But the damage to your reputation was done."

He nodded again, finding it hard to think, to speak, even to breathe when her fingers warmed his skin. "Nobody was ever charged with the crime, so the blame shadows me."

"Which is *ab in kopp*. Anyone who knows you should . . ." Her voice trailed off before she took a deep breath and said, "I'm sorry,

Elias. I can't accuse others of being shortsighted when I listened to the stories. I'm so sorry. I hope you can forgive me."

"There's nothing to forgive. You heard about the fire, and you wanted to make sure your brother didn't make the same mistakes."

"I should've asked you instead of jumping to conclusions."

The last ice around his heart cracked and melted. Trust Sarah Beth to accept responsibility when she believed she'd been wrong.

He did trust her, he realized. For the first time in longer than he could recall, he believed someone was on his side.

"Danki," he said.

Sarah Beth's sigh of relief drifted from her lips. Elias could have been furious because she'd let herself be swayed by what Mahlon had told her.

The sigh became a gasp when Elias lifted her hand off his arm and folded it within his much larger one. He put a gentle finger beneath her chin before he tilted it. Bringing her to her feet, he bent so his mouth covered hers before she had a chance to object.

She didn't want to object. His kiss was gentle and sweet, and she couldn't imagine anywhere else she wanted to be. Her hands slid up his sleeves and around his shoulders as she let the connection between them sweep her away. How often had she imagined being kissed? So many times, but in none of those dreams had she experienced such wunderbar joy.

When he raised his lips away, she didn't step back. She should have, but she didn't want this special moment to end. Reaching up, she traced his dark brows. He smiled as he kissed her hand. Wanting more of the delight, she guided his mouth to hers. He held her so close she couldn't tell if the rapid heartbeat belonged to her or him . . . or both.

She waited for him to say something after he finished the amazing kiss, but he grinned at her instead. She realized words weren't necessary as by common, unspoken consent, they walked toward where his buggy and hers were the last ones in front of the school. Though they didn't touch as they approached her siblings, she was as aware of him as if they were holding hands and her head was upon his shoulder.

Toby wasn't so reticent. "Well?"

"You may accept the part-time job offer as long as you continue to do your chores as you have been," Sarah Beth said, glad her voice sounded as if nothing untoward had happened, "and as long as you realize you won't be able to go to the shop when it's time for the next cutting of hay and when the corn has to come in."

"I will. I promise. I will." He gave her a quick hug before turning to Elias. Offering his hand again, he said, "You've got yourself a part-time helper."

Elias shook it. He surprised everyone, including Sarah Beth, when he said, "Toby, drive the others on ahead in Sarah Beth's buggy. Sarah Beth and I will follow you. We have a few other matters we need to discuss, and the ride back would be a *gut* time."

"Okay," Toby said, running to get Cinnamon.

The twins clambered into the buggy, but Cora gave Sarah Beth a studied wink before she got in as well.

Sarah Beth silenced her laugh at Cora's obvious satisfaction with her "matchmaking" efforts. Once Toby was driving the buggy toward the farm, she didn't hold in her laughter any longer.

Elias asked what was so funny. He chuckled too when she explained.

Their happiness lasted as long as it took them to reach Elias's shop. Seeing the Kings' buggy outside and the door of the shop hanging by one hinge, Elias brought his buggy to a quick stop.

Jumping out, Sarah Beth ran in, fearing what she was going to see. It was worse than she'd expected. Damage had been done to everything in the shop except the buggy. She wasn't sure why Abe's vehicle had been spared, but she was grateful it had been. It looked about ready to be returned to its owner.

"More footprints outside," Toby called. "Lots of them. They look like sneakers."

She saw him by the door. "They're getting more careless."

"Because we haven't stopped them," Elias said, folding his arms over his chest as he appraised the disaster. "Toby, at first I thought teens might be doing this. Have you heard anything?"

"Nothing." He gestured toward the floor. "This is worse than any teen prank."

Sarah Beth agreed. The worktable had been broken in half, and the tips of a half dozen smaller screwdrivers had been bent, making them useless. Other tools were ruined as well. Small pieces of wood were gathered close together in the middle of the floor.

She blinked on her tears. Someone had torn apart the birdhouse she'd made for Elias. The Red Sox logo had been gouged with a screwdriver so it was no longer visible.

Who would be so malicious?

Why?

Two questions she was no closer to answering than she'd been when his shop was first damaged. The vandals were growing more bold and destructive. She and Elias had to discover who they were and put a stop to their wanton mayhem before someone was hurt—or worse.

12

Elias dried the last bowl from breakfast and set it in the cupboard. Because he owned so few dishes, he needed to clean them after every meal. The kitchen looked empty without a shade on the window and nothing on the walls. A table and its sole chair were set between the sink and the big gas stove that had been made before his Grossmammi was born. The other three chairs were in the living room. One was for him to sit on and the other two held the oil lamp and a stack of magazines and catalogs he hadn't gotten around to reading.

It was a comfortable house, but it didn't feel like home. Not the way Sarah Beth's house did. Was it the steady *tick-tock* of the clock in her kitchen? More likely it was the unmistakable feeling of family that lingered like the aroma of baking bread. He couldn't say what created it. The easy chatter around the table or how Sarah Beth and her siblings worked together like a well-oiled pair of wheels?

At least, in the past three days, there had been no sign of the hooligans—he thought the name fit the vandals well—who'd wrecked his shop. He'd spoken with the district's deacon and the bishop after church on Sunday, and they urged him to contact the police.

He hadn't.

What if some other kid was arrested as he'd been? A kid who was trouble but hadn't had a hand in the destruction?

Elias doubted he could live with knowing he'd put someone else through what he'd endured twelve years ago. Yet if he didn't report the destruction to the police, the perpetrators could come back.

Or they might strike at the Kings' farm again.

The window gave him a clear view of Sarah Beth's house beyond the fields on the other side of the creek. Was he putting her in danger because he was trying to protect someone who might not exist? Toby had been sure the people who'd left those footprints weren't any teens he knew.

Wishing he could stop chasing his thoughts around in circles, Elias sat at the table and opened his accounting book. He drew out the stack of receipts he'd collected during the work on Abe's buggy. Sorting the pages, he wrote the pertinent facts in the book.

An hour later he pushed the paperwork aside. He was going to make a small profit on the work he'd done on the buggy, but it would take that profit and more to replace everything broken in the latest attack. He'd have to pay his rent from his savings again next month. The business needed to start making money to cover his expenses in another three months, or he'd have to find a cheaper place to live and work.

Again he looked at the Kings' farm. Would Sarah Beth be willing to rent him space in one of the farm's outbuildings? He didn't mind living rough, as long as he could keep the business going. Once he got through the next month, if nothing changed, he'd ask her.

Closing the book and setting it in a drawer, he reached for his straw hat and frowned. Where was the boy?

Anytime Toby was going to be late, he'd rush to the shop and alert Elias before hurrying home to do chores. On the rare occasions when Toby came early and found the shop door locked, he'd get Elias's extra key and let himself in.

There wasn't any sign of the lad.

Elias walked to his shop, scanning the road and the meadow between it and the Kings' farm. Both were empty.

Undoing the lock he hated having to use, he opened the back door. He took a single step into the shop and froze.

In front of him the center of the floor was empty.

The buggy he and Toby had spent weeks working on was gone.

He hurried to the spot where it'd been parked, stepping around scattered tools. He groaned. The mischief had escalated past vandalism. Someone had stolen a valuable buggy. To replace it for Abe Yoder would demand every penny Elias had earned in Hickory Meadows and more. In fact, he'd have to sell some of his tools, and that would be the end of his buggy shop.

Where was Toby?

Fear knifed him as he hoped the boy hadn't been in the shop when thieves came. Before he could alert the police, he needed to discover where his apprentice was.

As he rushed to the door and onto the road, running toward the covered bridge, one thought resonated through his head.

How am I going to tell Sarah Beth her brother is missing?

Everything looked as it always did as Elias approached the Kings' house. Laundry flapped in the breeze on the clothesline. Chickens pecked at the ground near their coop, and the soft lowing of a cow came from beyond the barn.

Opening the kitchen door, he saw that Sarah Beth and her friend Edith were in the living room. They were bent over a quilting frame, securing a quilt top onto it. Beside Sarah Beth's sewing machine, scraps of material and bits of thread revealed they'd just finished working there. Cora sat nearby, reading a book.

Edith noticed him first because she was facing the door. She must have said something across the quilting frame, because Sarah Beth motioned for him to come in without stopping her work.

He stepped into the kitchen and realized, for the first time since he'd been coming to the Kings' house, nothing was cooking on the stove. No luscious, enticing scents lured him into guessing what was bubbling on its top or baking in the oven.

"Oh, Elias!" Sarah Beth said with a strained laugh when she looked over her shoulder. "I didn't realize it was you."

He gasped when he saw how red the corners of her eyes were, as if tears had seared her skin. Why had she been crying? He wanted to pull her into his arms and reassure her that everything would be fine, that she'd never have another reason to cry.

Crossing the kitchen to stand in the doorway leading into the living room, he asked, "What's happened?"

"Toby and me. We argued."

"You've quarreled before."

She shook her head as she kneaded her hands together in her apron. "Those were spats, Elias. This time Toby refused to listen to *gut* sense."

"Teenage boys do that from time to time." He gave her a grin he hoped would ease her distress. "Where is he?"

"Isn't he at your shop?" She glanced at the clock on the kitchen wall. "He's usually there this time of day."

"I haven't seen him. I was expecting him an hour ago." He didn't say anything about the buggy, which was a lower priority than a missing boy.

Her eyes grew large. "Let me check the barn. Maybe he got delayed there." She rushed out.

As he started to follow, Edith put a hand on his arm, surprising him. "Be careful, Elias."

"Be careful?"

"With Sarah Beth. She appears to be as strong as the foundation of this house, but she isn't. I've known her our whole lives, and she's far more fragile than she lets anyone guess. She's afraid to do anything that will mean she'll never get the whole family living together under one roof."

"I know."

"*Gut.*" She lifted her hand away.

He nodded to Edith before striding from the house and across the yard to the barn. As he reached it, Sarah Beth burst out of the wide door.

"He's not here!" She looked around as if she expected Toby to pop out from behind a bush or tree in a bizarre game of hide-and-seek. Her voice was raw with anguish. "Where could he be?"

This pain was one piece of what it meant to belong to a family. He wished he could ease it for her, but he'd never been part of a real family.

All he could say was "Let's find him."

Sarah Beth dropped on one of the kitchen chairs and stared at her dew-soaked sneakers. She was glad Edith had offered to take Cora home with her so her sister didn't see Sarah Beth's despair. An agitated Cora would complicate the situation.

Where could Toby be? There wasn't an inch of the farm or its buildings she and Elias hadn't searched. They'd gone through the outbuildings near his house and shop as well.

Her stomach cramped as she thought of the empty shop. Elias had tried to halt her from going in, and she understood why when she realized Abe's buggy was gone. Not only the buggy, but they discovered when they checked the stable that Elias's harness horse, Wonder Boy, had vanished too.

"I don't know where else to look." She sighed.

"We can't put off contacting the cops any longer," Elias said.

She reached across the table and grasped his hand. "Not without talking to Uriah first. We can't involve Englischers until he's informed."

"If this is connected to the damage done here and to my shop—"

"I pray not."

"As I do." Elias's brown hair was plastered to his forehead with sweat. "We'll try one more thing. Who are Toby's best friends?"

She listed the three kids: cousins Ivan and Kenny Bawell and Orly Raber. "They've been inseparable from their first day of school together."

"First, let's check with them. If they can't help, we must speak with the bishop. We can't delay any longer."

"Let's go."

She wobbled as she stood up, exhausted with fear and worry. He tipped her head and gave her a quick kiss on the forehead. It was, she realized, as he hurried away to hitch her horse to the buggy, a promise. A promise to do everything possible to find Toby. And a promise his next kiss wouldn't be on her forehead.

Uriah Fry had been the local bishop for the district only the past few years. Before the lot had fallen on him, he'd served as the deacon in the other of the two districts he oversaw. Sarah Beth remembered the service when he'd been chosen. The lot was simple. After their previous bishop had died, the six ordained men of his two districts had taken part in the ritual. The ministers and the deacon from each district were in the lot, because the bishop needed to have had experience as an ordained man. The men prayed together before each was asked to select a copy of the *Ausbund* from six hymnals arranged on a table by two visiting bishops. In one was a slip of paper, and the man who selected that book was the new bishop. Prayers were spoken by the visiting bishops and the Leit asking God's guidance for the new bishop.

She'd been pleased when the lot fell on Uriah because he was known as a fair man. Still, she wished she didn't have to drive to his farm, which was in his other district beyond the Hickory Meadows crossroads.

Her hope that one of Toby's friends would be able to help had come to naught. One had been busy the entire day in the fields, and the second had gotten home minutes before from his work at his Onkel's sawmill. The third wasn't home, but his Mamm said he was staying with a cousin to help bring in the next cutting of hay.

After the third stop, Elias hadn't said anything when they returned to the buggy. He slapped the reins and drove toward Uriah's house.

Uriah's wife, Geneva, greeted them at the door. She was a short, plump Grossmammi with apple-red cheeks and streaks of gray through her black hair. As always, she was smiling, but she became serious when Sarah Beth stepped into the comfortable, pale yellow kitchen.

"I'll get Uriah," Geneva said after a single glance at Sarah Beth's face. "Wait here."

Within minutes the bishop, who was as round as his wife and no taller, came into the kitchen. He was wearing his gold-rimmed glasses, revealing he'd been reading when they arrived.

When Sarah Beth started to apologize for interrupting his late afternoon, he shook his head. "You could never be an imposition. I can tell from your faces something is amiss." He motioned toward the kitchen table. "Let's sit and talk."

She did and was glad when Elias sat beside her. Uriah took what she guessed was his usual place at the end of the table. When Geneva set fresh Kaffi and pieces of *Snitz* pie in front of them, Sarah Beth wasn't tempted by the lush, spicy scent of the dried-apple filling, which was one her favorites.

"*Was iss letz?*" asked Uriah.

Sarah Beth told the bishop—with help from Elias when she started to choke up—what was wrong.

Uriah's gaze cut from one to the other as they explained how they'd discovered Toby was missing as well as the buggy and Wonder Boy.

"A theft is always something to concern us," the bishop said, "but it's not like Toby to take off without letting someone know where he was going."

Sarah Beth felt her cheeks grow warm. Admitting she and Toby had had a quarrel wasn't easy, but she did. "I've gone over what we said, and I don't know what would cause him to run away like this."

"Siblings argue." He gave her a gentle smile. "That's one of the constants of the world. I'm sure you and Toby have had many disputes in the past."

"Plenty of times when I've needed to tell him not to do something he wanted to do. I'm not his Mamm, but I've had to play that role for two years."

"She's done a great job with him," Elias said, astonishing her because she didn't expect him to compliment her in front of the bishop.

Her heart was warmed by his praise. "I've done no more than any sister would."

"You've done all you can." His comforting touch on her elbow was gentle. It connected her to him and his strength and her eager longing to have his arms around her.

She was grateful he was there. To have to face Toby's disappearance alone would have been worse. For the past two years, she'd been responsible for her siblings. She hadn't realized how much of a difference it would make not to be alone while dealing with a crisis.

Uriah patted her other hand, also offering her solace, but it didn't set off fireworks within her as Elias's caress did. "I've got seven Kinder, so I know how hard it is to be a parent. It's more difficult, I'm sure, for you since Miriam died. You could use the help of an older man to be a guide for Toby."

"Elias has been doing that. He's been helping Toby learn the trade of fixing buggies."

"I'm glad to hear that. Danki for stepping up for a tough job, Elias." With a sigh, Uriah asked, "How long has Toby been missing?"

"Since before dawn this morning," Elias said.

Uriah chewed on his lower lip. "It would seem it's time to alert the Englisch authorities. They have methods and resources for finding people we don't. The boy said nothing to you of his plans to run away, Elias?"

"Nothing. He talked about how excited he was about the chance to ride in the buggy once it was finished. He was eager to see the results of his hard work." He rubbed his hand across his forehead, and she wondered if it was aching as hers was. "The boy has been an excellent apprentice, soaking up what I could teach him like a dry sponge in a wash bucket."

"Let's hope the lessons he's learned from you will help him make *gut* decisions." Pushing back his chair and coming to his feet, he added, "I'll call the police." He took his straw hat off its peg and opened the door. His phone, which was available for use when the Leit had an emergency, was in his barn. "Wait here. The police will want to speak to you."

She sensed Elias tensing beside her. His previous experience with the authorities had been traumatic. She prayed he—and Toby—would be all right.

13

The knock on the front door late that night startled Sarah Beth. The only time the house's front door had been used in the past few years was when they hosted a church Sunday or during Grossmammi Miriam's funeral.

Sarah Beth stood from where she'd been finishing securing the quilt top she and Edith had been working on to the quilting frame. Doing something had eased her nervous energy while she waited to hear that her brother had been found.

Two policemen had come to Uriah's house within a half hour of his call. They had asked plenty of questions, some making her uncomfortable when the officers sought reasons why Toby might have run away.

Her discomfort must have been far less than Elias's, but he'd shown no sign of it as he shared the information he had. When he had told them about the missing buggy and horse, he'd added that he had no idea who would take either.

She glanced at where he sat at the kitchen table, working on a puzzle in the newspaper. He hadn't made a mark on the page for the last ten minutes, so she didn't know if he was stumped or if his thoughts, like hers, were elsewhere.

The caller knocked again.

"I'll get it!" Cora announced, jumping to her feet.

Grabbing her sister's arm to keep her from rushing to the door, Sarah Beth asked, "Will you put the kettle on? We'll need hot water ready if our company wants something to drink, ain't so?"

Grinning because being allowed to use the stove top was an unusual privilege for her, Cora hurried to the stove. Several times in the past, she'd turned on a gas burner and left the kitchen, leaving a pot to boil dry.

"I'll watch her," Elias said.

With a nod of gratitude, Sarah Beth crossed the living room and opened the door.

She saw a tall silhouette with a raised hand and realized she'd interrupted the man as he was about to knock again. Her breath caught when she saw a marked state police car parked in front of her shop. She'd been so lost in her thoughts she hadn't heard it arrive.

The man on the porch shifted, and she could see his gray uniform with the keystone symbol on its sleeve. His hat had a wide brim, and the crown was pinched as if someone had squeezed the top between his fingers.

"May I come in, ma'am?" he asked. "I'm Paul Morgan. I'm with the state police."

"Of course. Come in." She stepped aside so he could enter the room, which suddenly felt much smaller because he was more than six feet tall and had shoulders that looked padded.

Footfalls sounded behind her. She knew Elias had walked into the living room.

The policeman took his hat off, revealing a nearly bald pate. He glanced at Elias but spoke to her. "Are you Sarah Beth King?"

She nodded.

"Toby King is your brother?"

"He is." Words exploded from her. "We've looked everywhere for him. I can't believe Toby has jumped the fence. He's never shown any inclination to join an Englisch community. He didn't take anything with him. Wouldn't he have taken something with him if he was going to jump the fence?"

"Ma'am—"

"Call me Sarah Beth, please."

The tall man smiled, and his forbidding appearance eased. "Thank you, Sarah Beth. Call me Paul."

"Danki."

"I'd like to speak with you about your brother." He looked again toward Elias. "If you wish this conversation to be private . . ."

"Elias is a family friend," she said, dismay flooding her as she wondered what the police officer had come to tell them.

Stepping forward, Elias introduced himself. "The boy works for me part time."

"You're the buggy maker?"

"I am." If Elias was surprised at what the policeman knew, he revealed no sign of it.

"The one who had a buggy go missing yesterday too?"

"Ja."

"Then, sir," the officer said, "what I have to say involves you as well as Sarah Beth." His gaze traveled from her to Elias. "Toby and the missing buggy have been found."

"Is he okay?" she asked, tightening her fingers together until they creaked.

"He's fine." He looked at Elias. "I can't say the same for your buggy."

"Buggies can be repaired," Elias said as Sarah Beth whispered a prayer of gratitude that her brother was unhurt. "Boys can't. What happened?"

"The usual, I'm afraid. Racing."

Sarah Beth's head jerked up, relief replaced by shock. "Toby was racing buggies?"

"Yes." Paul sighed. "It seems racing vehicles is one thing teenagers, no matter what their background, have in common. Wanting to prove who's got the fastest vehicle."

"Where's Toby?" she asked.

"At the accident site. He was bumped about but didn't need to be taken to the hospital. The other young man did, because he broke his left arm and leg."

"The horses?" Elias asked.

"Through the grace of God, neither driver was injured worse, and the horses are unhurt. Toby cut them loose before they could injure themselves in their panic. The boy showed good sense in that." He frowned. "If in nothing else."

"Where did the accident happen?" Sarah Beth asked.

"A few miles from here." Paul motioned toward the door. "I can take you there. I'm sure you'll want to see your brother. You're welcome to come too, Mr. Stutzman."

"Elias will do."

"That's right." The officer smiled. "I should have remembered you plain folks don't go in for titles. Not even mister or miss." Again he gestured toward the door. "Whenever you're ready."

Sarah Beth went to get her bonnet and Elias's hat from the pegs by the door, then halted. "I don't want to leave my sister alone."

"There's room for all of you in the cruiser. You'll have to ride in the back. I hope you don't mind."

"Of course not. Just please get us to my brother as soon as you can."

When Elias saw two more police cars as well as an ambulance parked by the side of the road, he wasn't surprised that the car that he and the King women rode in slowed to a stop. He waited until he heard the doors unlock. Paul had told them that the doors had to be opened by the driver, explaining that miscreants and criminals were kept behind the grille that separated the rear seat from the front. Elias hadn't said he already knew.

Elias stepped into the whirl of flashing lights, pausing to help Cora and Sarah Beth out. He didn't release Sarah Beth's hand and she held Cora's as they hurried toward where other officers were gathered.

He took a steadying breath, glad to be away from the close confines of the police car. If he hadn't wanted to see as soon as possible how Toby was doing and what damage the buggy had suffered, he would have avoided the vehicle. Sitting behind the grille had made him claustrophobic and brought back memories of the worst time of his life.

Bright beams from flashlights were aimed at the ditch on the other side of the road, but he didn't look there first. Where was Toby?

A slender form raced past him. Toby!

Sarah Beth flung her arms around her brother. He clung to her like a toddler.

"Toby, you shouldn't have disappeared," Cora chided her brother. "Why didn't you remember we don't go anywhere without telling one another? Do you know how much we've worried? It's not *gut* to be worried. It makes wrinkles. I read that, so it must be true. I don't want wrinkles, so let us know where you're going next time!"

Elias saw smiles, poorly hid, among the first responders as Cora continued to scold him. As always, she didn't withhold her opinions.

"Enough, Cora," Sarah Beth said.

Wanting to give them time alone, Elias walked through the crowd. These people, who hadn't paid attention to the Kings' reunion, were a mixture of Amish and Englisch. He guessed they lived along this back road. They were peering into the ditch.

Whether they'd guessed the buggy was his responsibility or not, several men stepped aside to let him see better. He sighed when he saw what had caught their interest.

Two buggies lay dented, with pieces cracked off them against the rocks of a miniature creek running toward a culvert that went under the road. He recognized what remained of the buggy he and Toby had worked so hard on. This morning he'd been ready to return it to Abe Yoder. Now it was in worse condition than when Abe had brought it in.

On its side in the ditch, the buggy's whole rear end had collapsed. Water from the tiny stream rippled through it. Not only would the upholstery need work, but everything wooden in the buggy would have to be replaced. He calculated the cost of repairs as he walked along the road to examine the buggy from different angles. The buggy was repairable—and he'd do it—but the damage done to his business might not be.

The other buggy was in worse shape because Abe's vehicle had landed on top of it, crushing its gray sides. He squatted and was relieved to see the passenger compartment was intact. Even so, the other driver could have suffered more than a broken leg and arm.

Paul had been correct when he said that Toby and the other driver had been spared by God's grace.

Turning, he walked to where Sarah Beth stood with her sister and brother. She struggled to smile, and he did the same. She was strong, but having her brother risk his life so foolishly had shaken her to her soul.

"Is the buggy ruined?" she asked.

Not caring about others surrounding them, he took her hand and squeezed it in commiseration. "Anything can be fixed." He turned to her brother but didn't release her soft fingers. He needed to hold on to someone he could depend on. That was Sarah Beth.

Toby didn't meet his eyes. "I'm sorry."

He sighed. "What possessed you to take the buggy and race it?"

"I wanted my friends to see how great it is after we fixed it."

"How great it *was*," Elias said in a clipped tone.

Toby seemed to crumble into himself, and Elias guessed the enormity of what he'd done had begun to sink into the teenager's hard head.

"What other *fun* do you have with your friends?" Elias asked.

"We race buggies when they can get their families' buggies. This was my first time to have one to drive because our buggy is old and rickety. That's all we do. Just race."

"Just?"

Toby hunched his shoulders and mumbled something.

Sarah Beth's voice was like velvet-covered steel when she said, "It's not *just*, Toby. You took someone else's buggy, a buggy the owner entrusted to Elias, and you have destroyed it. What other damage have you and your friends done?"

His head snapped up. "We don't go around destroying things." He glanced toward the ditch. "Not intentionally. It wasn't intentional tonight. Another buggy came out of nowhere, speeding right at us. If we hadn't pulled to the right, we would have hit him. Then our wheels got hooked together."

Paul had joined them. "Another buggy? You didn't mention that before. Just one more?"

"Ja." Toby looked down at the ground again.

"So that one wasn't racing you two or another buggy while driving toward you?" the policeman asked.

"I don't think so. I didn't see any other buggies."

"Why didn't you say something about this before?"

Toby flung out his hands. "That buggy is long gone. It didn't even slow down when we crashed to make sure we were okay. It sped away. What could you do now?"

"Find it!"

When Paul asked more about the buggy, the boy was only able to describe it as a gray buggy with a dark horse, which would fit most buggies in Lancaster County.

With a sigh the trooper said, "We'll see what we can find. The rest of Toby's statement has been taken, so if you want to take him home, I'll give you a ride. If you remember anything else, Toby, you need to let me know immediately. Don't worry if you don't think it'll help. Let us decide. Do you understand?"

"Ja. I mean, yes sir."

"You go with Paul, Sarah Beth, and take your brother and sister." Elias glanced at a shadowed silhouette in the nearby field. "I'll walk Wonder Boy home. He's going to need to be calmed down after what he's endured."

As the state trooper walked back to his fellow officers, Sarah Beth said, "Wait by the car, Toby. Take Cora with you."

"Are you coming?" her brother asked in not much more than a whisper.

"I'll be right there." She clamped her lips closed so hard Elias was surprised he didn't hear her teeth click.

As her siblings crossed the road to Paul's parked car, Elias said, "It'll be okay, Sarah Beth. Some lessons we must learn the hard way. I don't think Toby will be so idiotic again for a long time."

She yanked her hand from his and crossed her arms as if she needed a bulwark between her and the world. "Don't you understand, Elias? My Aenti and Onkel will use this as a reason to persuade everyone they are more fit to raise the twins than I am. If I can't keep one teen out of trouble, how can I handle three?"

"You've done a *gut* job with Toby. He simply made a mistake." He glanced around at the policemen. The bright lights cut through the dark sky instead of a smoky one, but he could have been back twelve years ago when he made what he hoped would always remain the biggest mistake of his life.

She sighed. "You're right. I need to focus on tonight's troubles. I can get my buggy and return for you and Wonder Boy."

"He's going to be skittish about a buggy tonight. Let's give him time to forget it."

"Will he?"

"I hope so." He shook his head. "I don't know if I ever will."

"Me neither."

Taking her by the hand again, he led her to the police car where her brother and sister waited. He stepped aside as Sarah Beth helped her sister in. Cora was overwhelmed by what had happened, and she hadn't uttered a word since seeing the damaged buggies.

Elias edged forward again when Toby started to get into the car. Putting his hand on the boy's arm, he jerked it back when Toby winced. The whole side of his arm was scraped, and Elias guessed from the stains on the torn shirt Toby had kept hidden from them that the boy's torso was as raw. Even so, what Elias was about to say would hurt the boy more.

"Don't return to the shop, Toby."

"What?" cried Toby.

"I don't want anyone working for me whom I can't trust. You can consider yourself fired."

"Fired?" Toby looked from Elias to Sarah Beth as if trying to decide which one might relent first.

"Ja, you stopped working for me the moment you took the buggy and my horse. I've got to be able to trust my employees."

"You can trust me." Tears glistened in the boy's eyes. "I won't do anything like borrowing someone else's buggy ever again."

"I know, because you aren't working for me any longer. I need to trust you." He shook his head to forestall Toby's reply. "Words are easy and cheap. I need to see actions that prove to me you're trustworthy."

"How can I show you if I can't work at the shop?"

"Your problem, Toby, not mine."

Sarah Beth motioned for her brother to get into the car before she went to Elias. Kissing him on the cheek, she said, "Danki. I don't know how I could have survived this day without your help."

"I was glad to help, but I hope I don't have to under the same circumstances ever again."

She glanced at the car and her brother. "I don't think you'll have to." She climbed into the car and shut the door.

Elias moved away when Paul got behind the wheel and started the powerful vehicle. As it drove away into the night, he walked in the opposite direction to retrieve Wonder Boy and walk him home.

For the first time in longer than he wanted to admit, he didn't rue anything he'd said or done tonight. He thanked the Lord for showing him that he had something to offer to Sarah Beth and her family. He dared to believe that *gut* might come from the disaster.

14

The next morning, Sarah Beth parked her buggy in front of Elias's buggy shop. She carried the basket she'd filled with cranberry muffins as well as a peach pie.

She'd discovered yesterday how nice it was to let someone else help her take care of her family. Elias had stayed with her until Toby was found. Since Grossmammi Miriam had died, she hadn't had anyone with whom she could discuss her fears as well as her hopes. She dared to believe Elias might be that person for her.

She was surprised to find the shop's door locked. Elias must not have come from the house yet.

Walking around the building, she headed to the large house. She paused on the porch. Should she knock or walk in? She'd never been to Elias's home before, and it didn't feel right to barge in without knocking.

He saved her from her quandary by opening the door and calling, "Gute Mariye! *Komm* in. I've got the sludge I call Kaffi on the stove, and you're welcome to some."

"You make it sound appetizing," she said with a laugh as she stepped into his spartan kitchen.

The room was neat, but there was little in it. A single cup and plate were dripping in a dish drainer balanced on one side of the sink, and the definite stench of burned Kaffi filled the air. A table that had seen better times stood in the middle of the large room with a single chair to keep it company.

She noticed that in the moment before her gaze slipped along Elias's smoothly shaven face. Her fingers tingled to trace those strong, handsome planes the way her eyes were.

To cover her delight, she held out the basket. "I brought something for you."

He took it and set it on the table. When he peeked under the red-and-white checkered cloth, he smiled. "Smells wunderbar." He raised his gaze to her. "What's in here?"

"A surprise," she said with a grin.

Lifting off the cloth, he picked up the birdhouse she'd set on one side. "You painted another one with the Red Sox logo! You didn't have to."

"I did."

"I was glad to help you find Toby."

She shook her head. "This doesn't have anything to do with my brother. I painted it days ago because I wanted to replace the broken one in your shop."

"In case someone walked in and wanted to get one for himself?"

Laughing at his teasing told her he hadn't bought her excuse for giving him the first birdhouse or this one, she said, "It can't hurt."

"Danki, Sarah Beth."

When he held out his arms, she slid into his embrace with ease. His kiss was light as it brushed her lips, but she couldn't mistake the longing in his eyes. He wanted to kiss her more deeply. She admired his restraint as she wished that he would give in to the temptation to sweep her senses from her with his fiery lips.

"That's a prelude," he said with a smile, "because here comes the tow truck with Abe's buggy."

Sarah Beth followed him outside in time to see a flatbed truck pull behind the shop. She gasped when she saw the battered buggy on the back. It looked far worse in the sunlight than it had last night.

While Elias went to open his shop so the buggy could be moved inside, she returned to the kitchen, emptied the pot, and began a new batch of Kaffi. She waited for it to percolate, put away the clean dishes, and wiped the counters. When she glanced into the living room, she saw it was as sparsely furnished as the kitchen.

Once the tow truck pulled away, she carried a steaming cup of the fresh Kaffi to Elias.

He took it and breathed in. "It doesn't smell like what I made. How do you make it so *gut*?"

"Practice. Elias, we've got extra furniture in the attic and in one of the storage barns on the farm. If you'd like to borrow any, feel free. It's nothing special. Just old family stuff."

"Old family stuff is special when you don't have any family." He stiffened. "Sorry, Sarah Beth. I shouldn't be repaying your kindness with grumbling."

"You don't have any family?"

"Not any like you have. My parents both disappeared soon after I was born, and I became a burden for everyone else."

"A Boppli isn't a burden. It's a gift."

He grimaced. "Not to hear my relatives tell it." Before she could retort, he gave what sounded like a very forced chuckle. "So you want to get rid of that old stuff, ain't so? I guess you don't like my decorating style."

"It's the plainest plain house I've ever seen." She blinked back the tears his story had brought to her eyes and tried to be as brave as he was. His pain and sense of abandonment were far deeper than she'd guessed.

"That's the perfect description." He opened the door and motioned for her to enter. "It suits me, but your offer of using the furniture is generous, and I may take you up on it."

She wanted to say, "Don't wait long because we might not be

on the farm much longer." She didn't. She hadn't decided whether to accept Mahlon's offer. *That* was what she wanted to discuss with Elias; it was the reason she'd come today.

"*Gut.*" She stared at the broken buggy.

Both rear wheels stuck out at peculiar angles. The front ones gave the buggy a knock-kneed, pigeon-toed stance. Water dripped from the interior, and the whole undercarriage was caked with mud. The dash was held in place by a single bolt and the wires connecting it to the battery beneath it. Rips across the upholstery made a strange pattern in the black velvet.

Looking at it, she could hardly believe Toby had emerged with only torn skin along his left side. It would be a very painful reminder of his mistakes for days. She'd spent more than an hour last night cleaning and smoothing salve over those abrasions. Cora had helped her bind them lightly, so air could reach them and he could move without causing more damage.

"Can you fix it?" she asked.

He set the birdhouse on the worktable he'd devised from a plank and two sawhorses. "I have to ask Abe if he wants me to attempt it. If he says no, I'll try to find him another buggy in the same condition as it was before Toby took it for a joyride. How's the boy doing?"

"He's uncomfortable and miserable, but I think he's learned his lesson. I'm grateful he wasn't hurt badly. Uriah let me know that the driver who was racing against Toby, his *gut* friend Orly, is home from the hospital."

"Isn't he the boy who was supposed to be visiting his cousin?"

She nodded and sat on the stool by his temporary worktable. "His parents are more upset about the lying than the racing, and I don't blame them."

"How about you?"

She opened her mouth to answer as the front door opened.

Toby stood in the doorway. His mouth dropped when he noticed her by the worktable.

She started to rise, but Elias put a hand on her shoulder. Knowing she shouldn't intrude between him and her brother, she folded her hands in her lap and said nothing. Toby knew how angry and disappointed she was in him already, and she wondered why he'd risked compounding that by sneaking to Elias's shop the moment she left the farm.

Though Elias had been curious about what she'd come to talk to him about, he'd known the best thing he could do was be patient and let her speak when she was ready. Now it would have to wait until her brother said what he had to say.

"Gute Mariye." Toby's voice was a soft whisper.

"Toby," Elias said in a clipped tone, though he saw the tears in the boy's eyes and knew how difficult it was for his former apprentice, "if you're here to plead for your job, it's not going to happen. I need a young man working with me, not a kid who doesn't think beyond the fun of the next minute. Do you know why I got into the business of repairing buggies?"

"No."

"Guess," ordered Elias.

Toby considered the question. "Because you like working with tools?"

"Part of it, but not the important reason." He motioned for Toby to take another stab at the truth.

"Because you like working with wood?"

"Another part of it, but what's the most important reason?"

Toby looked at Sarah Beth, then away. Elias wanted to tell him he was wasting his time. If she had any idea what Elias was alluding to, she wouldn't tell him. Toby needed to find the answer himself.

The boy tried a few more guesses. Each time Elias shook his head. Toby became more frustrated, almost spitting answer after answer.

After Toby's seventh attempt, Elias frowned. "You're never going to guess because you've got no idea what's important about buggies." Leaning his hands on the improvised table, he locked eyes with the boy. "It's safety. You look surprised, and I'm not surprised. All you care about is if it's faster than your friends' buggies."

"The other buggy—"

"Wouldn't have been a problem if you hadn't been where you weren't supposed to be."

Elias didn't give Toby a chance to react. He fired questions at the boy, quizzing him on the safety features of a buggy and why each one was important. At first Toby listed them in a surly voice; then he must have realized the point Elias was trying to make and became more reasonable.

"How many of those safety measures kept you and your witless friend from being hurt worse than you were?" Elias demanded.

"A lot of them." Toby raised his head and met Elias's gaze without flinching. "I know you fired me, but I wanted to bring you this, along with telling you again how sorry I am."

Elias hid his surprise as Toby held out a generous wad of bills. When Elias glanced at Sarah Beth, she showed no reaction either. He realized she was waiting to take her cues from him, trusting him to strike the right note with the boy.

Could he? He'd never been a parent. He'd had only a long list of people who didn't care what he did as long as he did it somewhere else.

Lord, he prayed, *help me to help Toby learn the lessons I've tried to teach him.*

Toby placed the bills on the table beside Elias. "It's not enough to pay for the repairs Abe's buggy needs, but it's everything I've got. Forty-five dollars. I want you to have it." Tears filled his eyes and must have burned his throat because his voice grew scratchy. "I'll pay you the rest, Elias. I promise I will. I've already talked to a couple of people about helping them with their chores."

"In addition to yours?" Elias's tone remained chilly. "You know your family relies on you."

"It'll be tough, but I'll make it work somehow."

"You hate farm chores," Sarah Beth murmured.

He turned to her. "I do, but I only have to work for those other farmers until I prove to Elias that he should rehire me." Hope returned to his face. "Ain't so?"

Elias nodded. He guessed the boy wanted to ask what it would take to earn that trust, but Toby mumbled about having to go or he'd be late for one of his new jobs.

Elias watched him leave. His shoulders were bent, but there was a determination in his steps Elias had never seen before. Sarah Beth's little brother was becoming a man, pushed into maturity by his mistakes.

Just as Elias had been.

As soon as the door closed behind Toby, Elias relaxed from his taut stance. He picked up the money and fingered the bills, knowing how long it must have taken for a boy to save so much. The forty-five dollars must have represented several years of squirreling away the cash a little bit at a time.

Dropping it on the table, he said, "You did a *gut* job with him, Sarah Beth. That couldn't have been easy for him."

"I had no idea he'd saved that much money from the odd jobs he's done for the past few years."

"Didn't he give you part of what he earned?" He was astonished.

When he was Toby's age, whoever he'd been living with had insisted that he turn over everything he had made in exchange for food and a bed. How different his life would have been if one person had treated him with the kindness and respect Sarah Beth showed her brother!

She was an amazing woman with a giant heart that seemed to have room for everyone within it. Through the losses she'd suffered and the challenges she'd faced, she'd remained filled with hope and love and faith. She didn't deserve a messed-up man like him in her life. She should have someone who could ease the weighty burden of responsibility off her shoulders, not add to it.

"No," she said, and he knew she was oblivious to the thoughts flaying him. "I wanted Toby to have money he'd earned to fall back on when—if—we sell the farm."

Her words brought him up short. His emotions focused like a laser as fury exploded inside him. It wasn't rational, but he couldn't halt it. "You're considering selling your farm? Why on earth would you do something like that?"

"Because someone is interested in buying it."

"Someone? Who?"

She started to answer, then clamped her lips closed. "I probably shouldn't say until we come to an agreement."

"And then you'll just sell? Do you even have anywhere else to go? Sarah Beth, have you lost your mind?"

Sarah Beth was surprised by the shock and bitterness in Elias's voice. Why was *he* bitter? She was the one losing everything her family had worked for through many generations.

"I don't know if I have any choice." She fought the tears she was determined not to shed. "It's clear Toby has no interest in farming. With the money from selling the farm, it'd be possible for us to live on what I earn from my crafts."

"And bring your little sisters to live with you?" No warmth eased his tight tone.

"That's my dream."

"How will you provide for the five of you without the farm?"

She had made a lot of plans and discarded them, but talking to Elias reminded her about his landlord. "Maybe Harry Fitzgerald would rent me a place. Maybe he still has that empty store in Strasburg. It must have had a place for you to live if you considered moving there, ain't so?"

"Upstairs," he said reluctantly.

"*Gut,*" she said, trying to put a reasonable plan together. She knew she should think about it more before making any decisions, but the words, once started, poured out of her like a flood. "We can live upstairs, and I can open a shop and sell my birdhouses. Edith is interested in putting her quillows in the store, and several other women contacted me about selling their handicrafts when I was going to open the shop by the house. If I take their needlework on consignment, it's possible I could make enough to feed us and pay the rent. The twins can help me with the store after school and on Saturdays."

"You've got it planned out, don't you?"

Her temper frayed. Why was he talking to her like this? Each of his words was aimed at driving her away. Was that what he wanted? Why? He should be pleased she had an option to reunite her family. When she'd first told him of her plan to open the shop, he'd been enthusiastic and offered to help her. What had changed?

"I have to have a plan, Elias. If I don't try to make us a family again, who will? Toby is a boy, and Cora will never live on her own.

The twins are only twelve. The community would step in to help, but that would mean us being separated again. I want my family *together*. Nothing—most especially not a farm—is worth more to me. Why can't you understand?"

When he flinched as if she'd slapped him across the face, she gasped. She'd struck him, not with her hand but with her words, in the spot within him that had been torn apart by indifference and by being made to feel as if he didn't belong anywhere.

His voice was taut again when he asked, "Have you come to a deal with your potential buyer?"

"No, Mahlon . . ." She flinched. She hadn't intended to reveal that Mahlon was the one who was pressuring her to sell the farm.

"Mahlon? Mahlon Yoder? You're planning to sell your farm to *him*?"

"Why not? He's a member of the Leit, and he says he wants to be a farmer rather than work in his Daed's store. He wants to give me a more-than-fair price for it. I'd be a fool not to take his offer."

"Or a fool to take it," he said grimly.

"What do you mean by that? Give me one *gut* reason why I shouldn't sell him the farm and have my family back together again."

Elias stared at her for a long moment before saying, "I'm not sure I can give you one *gut* reason, Sarah Beth."

"Then why did you say I'd be a fool to take his offer?"

Again he said nothing, and the silence grew between them. She saw sorrow and pain in his eyes. This conversation hadn't gone as she'd hoped. She'd hurt him. That had been the last thing she'd wanted to do.

Standing, she walked out of the shop before she could say something that would hurt him—and her—more. She didn't look back, because she feared everything she'd thought she'd found with him was lost again.

15

How could a week feel as if it'd lasted a lifetime?

Sarah Beth sat across from Edith at the quilting frame and tried to keep her depressing thoughts hidden. Her needle went through the quilt top and into the cotton batting and the plain blue fabric providing the base for the quilt. The backing was wider and longer than the quilt top, so it was pinned up and over it to create a pretty edging.

Rain battered the living room windows, and Cora was curled up in a chair with one of her favorite books. Luann and Lovina played cards at the kitchen table. Sarah Beth had hoped to have a picnic with her sisters, but the weather was as low and grim as her spirits. To keep the girls from being bored, she'd had them help her make a casserole for supper. It was in the oven, and the aroma of tomato and spices wafted through the house. It would be ready when Toby returned home from his work on a nearby farm and finished milking their own cows.

"Are you going to sit there and say nothing all afternoon?" Edith said, not looking up from her tiny stitches.

"I don't have much to say."

Cora put down her book. "She and Elias had a fight. Elias and I never fought when we were walking out together."

"A fight?" Edith's needle paused. "Well, that explains why you're as silent as a stone, Sarah Beth. What did you argue about?"

"Elias got upset about something I said." She knew he'd been unhappy that she might sell her farm, but that didn't explain the ferocity of his reaction. "I was shocked, and it went downhill from there."

"So you said something you wish you hadn't." Edith shrugged as she smiled. "Everyone's done that, Sarah Beth. Even Darryl and me."

"I didn't think you ever argued."

Her friend laughed before sticking her needle into the fabric and leaving it there. When she raised her gaze from their quilt project, her eyes were twinkling with amusement. "*What* gave you that idea? Darryl and I argue as much as any other couple." She chuckled again. "More since we've been making decisions for the wedding."

"I've never heard either of you say a cross word to the other."

"We don't air our dirty laundry in front of others because our disputes are always about something ridiculous. Something we quickly realize." She wagged a finger at Sarah Beth. "We aren't talking about Darryl and me. We're talking about you and Elias."

"There isn't any me and Elias."

With a snort of half laughter and half disagreement, Edith said, "Well, that'll be news to everyone else in Hickory Meadows. You two have been mooning over each other almost as blatantly as someone else in this room did before she dumped Elias for another boyfriend." She gestured with her head toward Cora, though her words had been self-evident.

"What others believe is true doesn't mean something *is* true."

Edith waved aside her feeble protest. "So what made him change?"

She shrugged. "One minute he was complimenting me on how well I've raised Toby and the next he was furious."

"There must have been something else between his compliment and his anger."

She strained to remember the sequence of the conversation. "He asked me if I was planning to sell the farm."

"What did you tell him?"

Standing, Sarah Beth motioned for her best friend to follow her onto the porch. She didn't want her sisters hearing what she had to say.

Water ran off the roof and splattered in the flower beds Cora had planted with annuals earlier in the week. The bright orange and red flowers danced as raindrops struck their blossoms and leaves.

Edith sat on the swing. "So what did you tell him?"

"I had to consider selling so I'd be able to give the twins what they need." She sighed. "Or what my Aenti and Onkel insist they need, though they've never specified what that is."

"They don't have to." Edith hesitated. "Sarah Beth, I don't like to speak ill of anyone, but it's been obvious to me what's going on. Your Onkel and Aenti don't want the twins to come home because Luann and Lovina give them what *they* need. Kinder."

"I know."

"Why haven't you asked Uriah to speak to them on your behalf? As our bishop, he's the one to mediate such issues."

"He's busy and—"

"Ask him! He can help you."

Sarah Beth sighed. Edith was right, and Sarah Beth wondered why she hadn't sought the bishop's assistance before.

Because you wanted to prove you could do it on your own, came the answer from her conscience. *Is your Hochmut worth losing your sisters?*

She leaned against the railing as her friend sat on the swing. "Danki, Edith. You're a *gut* friend."

"So let me help you with Elias. I see how upset you are." She tapped her fingers on the arm of the swing. "Look at it from his perspective. He's afraid you'll move away and he won't see you again."

"Toby . . ."

Edith gave another indelicate snort. "Ja, Toby would miss working at the shop, but *you* are the one who will, if you move away, be really, really missed by Elias."

"I told him I hoped to move to Strasburg."

Edith stood and put her hands on Sarah Beth's shoulders. "It's too far away when he wants you closer. Think about that!"

Sarah Beth remained on the porch when her friend went inside. Gazing at the silvery curtain of rain, she considered Edith's words. Was Elias hurt because he yearned to have her closer? How much closer? Did he want her in his arms as she ached to be?

She wasn't sure of the answers to those questions, but she was certain of one thing: She'd fallen in love with her irascible neighbor. Yet she must fulfill the promise she'd made to her family to bring them together. Was she going to have to sacrifice one love for another?

Staying away from her and her family is the best thing I can do for Sarah Beth.

No matter how many times Elias had repeated that since Sarah Beth had walked out of his shop eight days ago, his heart refused to believe it. He'd come to Hickory Meadows to escape his past. If she sold her farm to Mahlon, his past could be moving right next door; he'd heard the shopkeeper's son was walking out with Vera Swartzentruber.

Maybe he should let his landlord know he was interested in the property near Strasburg. It would get him away from Vera, who was a constant reminder of her brother and the disaster that had changed Elias's life. But leaving would take him from the district where he'd been made welcome among the Leit.

Worse, though, was the fact Sarah Beth and her family would be living far away. He had to be happy for her that she'd have the twins at home again.

If he stayed and convinced her to do the same . . .

An ironic laugh burst from him like a donkey's bray. Whether either of them stayed or not, the bottom line remained the same. He wasn't worthy of a wunderbar woman like Sarah Beth King. He should have told her the truth from the beginning. It would have kept their lives from getting entangled and their hearts hurt.

He had no doubt he'd broken her heart. Her face had displayed pain before she left his shop, and she hadn't returned. He knew he must fight his heart's urging to tell her the truth and beg her forgiveness.

"Elias! Elias, are you in the shop?"

The shout brought him from his reverie. Putting down the tools he hadn't used for the past fifteen minutes while lost in frustrated thoughts, he stood from behind the buggy that was beginning to look less like a pile of parts and more like a proper vehicle.

Toby!

What was the boy doing at the shop before midday? Had he come to ask for his job again? Elias had to admire the kid's persistence, but Toby needed to recognize the breadth of his mistakes. Eight days hadn't given the boy time enough to contemplate them.

Or had it? Elias had had more than enough time to consider his.

"Oh, Elias! I'm glad you're here!" The boy rushed to him, but paused an arm's length from the buggy. He seemed unsure what to do with his hands and arms as he rocked from one foot to the other.

"I'm here, but you shouldn't be. Does Sarah Beth know where you are?"

"She sent me to tell you she needs to talk with you. Now!"

His heart did a jig in his chest, and he tried to pay no attention to it, the same way it had ignored his attempts to put Sarah Beth out of it for the past week.

"Has something happened to the farm stand or shop?" Elias asked.

Toby shook his head. "Komm on! Sarah Beth said she'd explain." The boy looked ready to burst, but he didn't add anything else.

Elias reached for his straw hat and set it on his head before following his one-time apprentice out of the shop. Pausing long enough to lock the door, he jogged after Toby across the covered bridge.

When he followed Toby into the house, nothing looked amiss. The twins were at Sarah Beth's sewing machine, working on what looked like a new dress. Cora chopped wizened carrots at the kitchen table with a book propped against a bowl. Whatever was happening hadn't upset her, but then she could lose herself in her reading and be oblivious to everything going on around her.

Sarah Beth came from the living room, her lovely face full of dismay. The happy color of her dark purple dress couldn't counteract her dim eyes and tight lips.

"What's going on?" Elias asked in lieu of a greeting.

"Sit down," Sarah Beth said.

He looked from her to Toby, whose expression was as grim as Sarah Beth's. Wanting to ask again what was going on, he pulled out the closest chair. She wouldn't answer his questions until she was ready.

"What's going on?" He hoped he didn't have to repeat those words too many more times before someone gave him an answer.

"Edith sent Adam, one of her younger brothers, here. Uriah was visiting her parents' house earlier this morning. While he was there, a policeman from the county sheriff's office came looking for him."

"He wanted to speak with our bishop?" He was glad he was sitting because he wasn't sure if his knees would have kept him erect as he registered the shock of her words. Somehow he managed to ask, "Why?"

She shook her head. "He wants to find you, and he guessed Uriah would be able to point him in the right direction."

"What's his name?" he asked as a feeling of coldness sank deep into his bones.

"Deputy Rodriguez. Do you know him?"

"Ja," he said with a resigned sigh.

"From before?" she asked.

"Ja." He glanced at her sisters and brother, knowing that keeping the past a secret wouldn't help anything. "Twelve years ago, Martin Rodriguez was a rookie cop involved in the investigation into the barn fire where my phone was found. He came to the house where I was living with a distant cousin and arrested me, taking me away in his cruiser."

Toby and the twins gawked at him, but Sarah Beth's expression didn't change.

"I told Adam to send the policeman here." She started to reach out to him, but pulled her hand back. "I thought you'd prefer to have friends with you when you spoke to him."

He was sure his clobbered heart took a beat for the first time in a week as he discovered, no matter how many sharp words they'd exchanged, that the Kings, led by Sarah Beth, were ready to stand beside him. All he could say was "Danki."

Before anyone replied, a knock on the front screen door made him flinch, but he didn't jump up and flee. He wasn't a scared teenager any longer. He was a man with a shameful past, but he was done running away from it.

"Go upstairs," Sarah Beth ordered her siblings.

The twins started to protest, but when Toby and Cora led the way, they obeyed without a single question or comment.

When their footfalls resounded overhead, she went to the door and opened it. "Hello. Please komm in."

Elias recognized the man. In the past decade, the tall, painfully thin man hadn't put on much flesh. Rodriguez took off his hat, which was the same dark color as his uniform. A huge patch with a star on his left sleeve identified him as a county deputy sheriff.

Elias stood up. "Deputy Rodriguez, how can I help you?" He wondered if either the cop or Sarah Beth believed his self-possessed tone.

"We need to have a chat." He smiled when he looked at Sarah Beth. "Thank you for agreeing to let me meet Elias here." His voice was deep for such a lean man.

Sarah Beth led the way into the kitchen and motioned for them to sit at the table. She went to the stove and poured Kaffi. After setting cups in front of them, she filled a plate with warm snickerdoodles and chocolate chip cookies.

As she offered Rodriguez the plate, Elias noticed Toby standing on the stairs, halfway up. He was trying to hear what was being said in the kitchen. He hoped that when this discussion was over, the boy would understand why Elias had been tough on him. He didn't want Toby to try something bigger and badder. If Elias had had someone to help him learn the tough lessons, they wouldn't be sitting here now with a deputy sheriff.

Sarah Beth noticed her brother too, and she motioned for him to come down but not say anything. Toby nodded when introduced to the deputy sheriff. He sat beside Elias.

When Sarah Beth sat on his other side, Elias asked, "What do you want to chat about?"

"There's been another fire." Rodriguez's mouth twisted. "Actually, there have been six or seven fires at the farm in the years since the one you were arrested for."

She watched Elias's face. He was struggling to hide his thoughts, but his clasped hands matched the tension in his shoulders.

"You can't believe I had anything to do with them," Elias said. "I left the area right after I was freed, and I haven't been back."

"No, I don't think you're involved."

"Then why are you here?"

"To bring you up to date on what's happened at Solomon Yutzy's farm. Solomon has never been a patient man." He paused to take a sip of Kaffi before adding, "I have learned he's been having small fires in his hay barn every spring. Fires caused by spontaneous combustion."

"Because he didn't let his hay dry and put it in the barn green?"

The sheriff nodded.

Sarah Beth glanced from one man to the other. "Doesn't Solomon spray his hay?"

The officer gave her a blank look.

Toby jumped in, surprising her, because she hadn't thought he'd say anything in front of a cop after the incident with buggy racing. "Farmers use commercial sprays to keep damp hay from building the heat that sets it on fire."

"Obviously Solomon didn't, because the latest fire burned his barn to the ground. It was caused by spontaneous combustion." Deputy Rodriguez cleared his throat. "In the wake of these fires Solomon has had year after year, fires we've learned about after this year's, I've been wondering if your scorched cell phone was the cause or simply a victim of a fire started by improperly stored hay."

"You know what I'm going to say."

Rodriguez smiled coolly. "Exactly what you said twelve years ago, right? You lost your phone and had no idea where it was until the ruined one was found."

"It was the truth then and it is now."

Sarah Beth held her breath as she looked from one man to the other. They were regarding each other like two bulls facing each other across a fence. Neither was willing to show any emotion, but neither was willing to back down.

"However," the deputy sheriff said, "that leads to other questions nobody, including me and you, thought to ask twelve years ago."

"What questions?"

"Are you sure you lost your phone in the hayloft?"

"I must have. How else would it have been found there?"

"*That* is the critical question."

Sarah Beth almost choked as she asked, "Are you saying someone found Elias's phone and put it in the hayloft?"

The deputy affixed her with his steady gaze and nodded. "Yes, but I don't have any proof. It seems everyone has known for years Solomon Yutzy has had a multitude of small fires as well as the two big ones. What better way to get someone in trouble than connecting them to something that's going to happen sooner or later?" He leaned forward, his arms folded on the table. "If you're innocent as you've always claimed—"

"Which he is!" Toby blurted out.

The deputy said with a smile, "You've got good friends, Elias."

"I do." He squeezed Sarah Beth's hand under the table.

"You've got good friends *here*, but someone may have wished you trouble twelve years ago." He leaned forward, his smile gone. "Who was angry enough at you to set you up back then, Elias?"

16

Elias stumbled over his futile attempt to answer the deputy sheriff. Did Rodriguez honestly think that someone had put his phone in the barn so Elias would be blamed once the hay started to burn?

"Who had the opportunity?" the deputy sheriff asked.

"Any of the Hooligans." He listed their names.

Rodriguez frowned. "Swartzentruber? I didn't realize the deacon's son was a member of your running-around gang."

"He was, but he avoided getting blamed for our pranks."

"In other words, the deacon stepped in and made sure his son's name was never mentioned." He waved a hand. "No need to say more, Elias. This isn't my first rodeo . . . No, that's not right. It isn't my first *frolic* with your people."

Elias couldn't help smiling at the deputy's jest, and he heard Toby's snicker behind his hand. A glance at Sarah Beth revealed her eyes were twinkling merrily. Oh, how he'd missed seeing the happy glow in them!

The sound of horse hooves and metal wheels came through the screen door, and they looked as one toward the front of the house. Excusing herself, Sarah Beth went to see who was coming up the lane. When the cop followed, Elias did as well with Toby tagging after them.

Two buggies were pulling to a stop close to the house. Elias watched Sarah Beth square her shoulders as she led the way onto the front porch. He watched as four men stepped from the buggies, each of them looking uneasily at the police car.

He identified the four men. Uriah, their bishop, had driven Abe Yoder, one of the ministers in the district, to the farm. Instead of the deacon who usually appeared when a member of the Leit had strayed off the path the faithful walked, the other men were younger, closer to his own age.

Mahlon Yoder strode toward the house, keeping pace with his Daed. Elias was shocked to see that the other younger man was Darryl Glick, the man Sarah Beth's best friend intended to marry.

Glancing at her, he saw that her face was serene. Was that an honest expression or was she hiding her dismay?

Toby wasn't as circumspect. "What are they doing here? If Abe's angry about his buggy . . ."

Elias put a calming hand on the boy's shoulder. "Let's listen to what they have to say before we jump to any conclusions." Advice he needed to take himself. "I would say they believe, as I do, that you've learned your lesson the hard way and won't make the same mistake again."

The boy stood straighter. "So I can return to the shop?"

"We'll have to wait and see." He expected Toby to protest, but the boy nodded as understanding bloomed in his dark eyes.

Toby looked at the men approaching the house, and a shiver ran up his spine.

"You don't have to stay," Elias said.

"Ja, I do. I'm the man of the house." He raised his chin as he walked to the center of the porch and stopped by the stairs. "*Wie geht's?*" he called in greeting.

"We're doing well, Danki," Uriah said as he came to the house. "We thought we would stop by and make sure everything is okay."

"It is," Toby said at the same time as his sister.

Sarah Beth stepped forward and put her arm around her brother's shoulders. Elias saw her astonishment when she had to adjust her arm upward because Toby had shot up in the short time Elias had known him.

"Would you like to come inside? I have Kaffi on, and there are cookies." She smiled at Uriah. "Your favorites. Snickerdoodles."

Deputy Rodriguez paused as a voice came from the radio device hooked to his shoulder. "Excuse me. I've got to take this." He walked toward his car.

Mahlon took advantage of the distraction to push past his Daed and Darryl to stand beside the bishop. "Sarah Beth, this isn't your business."

"It is if you're standing on my land." She tilted her chin. "It's still my land, Mahlon. I know that as surely as I know Elias Stutzman is a *gut* man, no matter what happened in the past." When Mahlon started to open his mouth, she hurried to say, "Or didn't happen!"

"You're ab in kopp, Sarah Beth, to trust him." He ignored the glare from his Daed, a clear warning to be quiet.

"No she's not!" Toby looked from Elias to the bishop. "I trust him."

"You're just a boy," said Mahlon with a sneer that vanished when his Daed hissed something in his direction.

"I am a man." There was no belligerence in Toby's words. They were as calm as his sister's. "I've graduated from school, and in our community that means I have the obligations of a grown man. I should have the right to speak my mind like a man too."

"Toby," Sarah Beth cautioned, "angry words won't change minds."

"His words aren't angry," the bishop said with his quiet dignity. "They are the words of a *man*." He emphasized the word as he looked at each of the other men in turn. "A man who believes what he's saying. No man should be denounced for the fire in his soul that moves him."

Mahlon refused to be silenced. "Fire is why we're here."

"There have been questions raised, Elias. They need to be answered." Abe sighed.

"I want them answered too," Elias replied.

The door opened behind him, striking him. He heard a sharp intake of breath from Sarah Beth when Cora walked out with the twins in tow. Would Cora say something to compound the already-tense situation?

Everyone waited for the young woman to speak, but she grabbed Lovina and Luann by the hand before walking to Sarah Beth.

"Uriah, we're always supposed to tell the truth, ain't so?" Cora asked.

"Ja, Cora, that's true."

"I'll tell you the truth. Our family trusts Elias," Cora said.

The twins nodded, their eyes wide.

"We stand with our family," Lovina said.

"Our whole family." Luann smiled as she took Sarah Beth's hand in her other one.

Toby moved beside Elias, who was shocked when he felt a small hand curve into his. He saw Lovina holding his hand and smiling at him.

Suddenly the accusations meant nothing. This loving family's kind gesture meant everything. He glanced over her head to see Sarah Beth's unsteady smile. In her eyes he saw the answers to the questions he'd never voiced. She believed him. As important, she believed *in* him and what he was now and dreamed for in the future.

Her family now stood beside him and defended him from rumors and innuendo. A family. Not a family truly his own, but a family who welcomed him within it.

"If I may speak . . ." Sheriff Rodriguez had returned, unnoticed. Uriah nodded. "Please do."

"I think you gentlemen are under the impression I'm here to arrest Elias Stutzman because of the fire in Solomon Yutzy's barn."

"The fire Elias was arrested for starting?" asked Mahlon.

"And released when there was no evidence?" added Darryl, coming to Elias's defense. "Why are you arguing with the facts, Mahlon? The investigation was over years ago. I'm sure the statute of limitations has run out on the incident, even if someone was guilty."

Those words earned a blistering scowl from Mahlon. "When did you study law, Darryl?"

"Let the deputy talk," the bishop said in a conciliatory tone.

"More recent fires have caught my attention." Deputy Rodriguez smiled as he turned to the bishop. "If I gave you the wrong idea of why I wanted to find Elias right away, Uriah, I apologize. I should have taken time to explain that the fire today has raised questions about the fire twelve years ago. I'm finished here, so is there somewhere you and Abe and I can talk without interruption?" He glanced meaningfully at Mahlon.

"My house," Uriah said. "You know the way, Martin."

The deputy nodded. "I do."

Elias didn't move as the policeman went to his car, and Uriah motioned for Abe to precede him to his buggy. Darryl started to follow, then turned and yanked on Mahlon's sleeve. Mahlon shot one more glare at the porch before he left too. Within minutes the yard was empty.

Sarah Beth went with her family into the house, urging Elias to join them at the table.

Elias nodded, but he remained on the porch for a few minutes. This wasn't over. Some sense that had no name warned him. His past wasn't finished with him.

Not by a long shot.

Sarah Beth rolled over in her bed and snuggled her face into her pillow. A light had thrust into her dream of walking hand in hand with Elias along the creek between the farm and his shop. It wasn't just a dream.

They'd taken a walk that evening after supper while the long spring twilight turned the sky from blue to black and welcomed the stars to shine.

It had been a celebration because Elias had gone with her to talk to Uriah after supper. The bishop had listened to her explanation of why the twins should be with their family. He hadn't promised anything, but he had agreed to speak with her Onkel and Aenti. She prayed it would help bring Lovina and Luann home for *gut*.

Raising one eyelid, Sarah Beth wondered who was up in the middle of the night. It must be one of the twins because they were no longer familiar with the house when it was dark. Toby didn't need a flashlight to find his way downstairs. Sarah Beth had seen Cora's earlier in the bathroom.

Then she realized the light wasn't coming from the hall. It was coming through the window.

Pushing herself to sit, though she was entangled in sleep, Sarah Beth forced both eyes open. Had someone driven a car into the lane?

She came awake when she saw the orange glow flickering.

Fire!

She ran to the window. In horror, she stared at flames licking the almost-finished shop.

Grabbing her bathrobe and pulling on her sneakers, she didn't bother to tie either as she ran into the hallway. As she reached the top of the stairs, she heard cries of dismay behind her.

Her siblings poured from their bedrooms. She told Toby to get the hoses from the barn. She sent Cora and the twins to find every bucket they could.

As she raced out the front door, she kept glancing at the fire. She ran into a shadowed form who was dragging a hose from the reel on the front of the house.

Elias!

Switching on the hose, he aimed the water at the flames. "Don't go any closer!" he called. "Have you called for help?"

"Not yet."

"Go!"

"It's *my* shop!"

"I know that! You say you trust me, Sarah Beth. Trust me."

Knowing she was letting panic overwhelm her *gut* sense, she ran toward the phone shack sitting on the property line between her farm and the one next door. She threw the door open and grabbed the phone from where it sat on a small shelf. She hit the button and held it to her ear.

No dial tone. *What . . . ?*

She grappled with the base unit, tipping it toward her to make sure it was properly attached. A length of wire popped out from behind the shelf and almost struck her.

The phone line had been cut!

Fear spurred her feet as she ran across the lawn to find Toby stooding where Elias had stood. She saw a form moving near the fire and heard the sizzle of water on flames. Elias had shifted to fight from a different angle.

"Did they say how long?" her brother asked.

"I couldn't call. Someone cut the wire."

"What?" Disbelief crossed his face.

"Toby, you're going to have to ride to the nearest house with a phone and call 911 from there."

Cora stepped out of the darkness. "I'll use my cell phone. Call 911. Okay, Sarah Beth?"

Wondering how and when her sister had gotten a cell phone, she didn't have a chance to answer before Toby handed Sarah Beth the hose. He snatched the phone from Cora's hand and stabbed in the emergency number.

"My phone!" cried Cora. "I call."

"You make the next call," Sarah Beth said to ward off an argument.

Elias's abrupt bellow was so loud she heard it above the crackling flames. Shoving the hose into Cora's hands and telling her to keep it aimed at the fire, though the thin stream of water didn't seem to be helping much, Sarah Beth ran toward him.

Was he hurt? Had he tried to go into the building in a foolish attempt to save her birdhouses and Edith's quillows?

Please, God, let him be safe. He doesn't need to prove to me he's a gut *and decent man.*

A form jumped from the darkness, which was blacker away from the eye-searing blaze. The woman swung her arm.

Sarah Beth tried to duck, but she hadn't realized that the woman held something. A branch struck her. Twigs and leaves sliced across her face but kept the full power of the stroke from hitting her. Her ears rang with the concussion, and she was knocked back several steps.

A motion from the corner of her eye alerted her. The woman raised the branch for another blow, then ran.

Sarah Beth sent a prayer up to God for strength. She hoped He'd understand why she must fight. She couldn't let the woman turn her fury on her siblings.

She threw herself forward as she used to when she played baseball at school. Instead of sliding into second base, she stretched out and caught the fleeing woman by the ankles.

The woman fell to the ground. Hard. She didn't move.

Coming to her knees, Sarah Beth reached to turn the woman over. She paused when she heard shouts from the twins on the front porch in the seconds before the shriek of a siren cut through the pounding in her skull. The firefighters! Toby must have reached 911.

She risked a glance toward the house and saw Cora jumping and pointing toward the shop. In the light from the flames, two forms struggled. She heard the unmistakable sound of flesh against flesh and a moan of pain.

Wanting to go help Elias, she knew she couldn't let the woman get away. She bent to look more closely at the woman's face.

"Vera!"

Her astonishment doubled when, from the shadows, Elias said, "And Mahlon. Our firebugs lingered too long to admire their handiwork, and they couldn't get away without us seeing them. When we got too close, they attacked."

He stepped forward, his hand gripping Mahlon's coat. His own was ripped, and both men were covered in dirt.

"I stopped him from running away." A smile played across Elias's expressive lips. "Like you stopped Vera, I'd say."

"She knocked her head against the ground when she fell," Sarah Beth said.

Mahlon let out an anguished cry. "My sweet, sweet Vera!"

"She's going to be fine," she said. "Here comes help."

A police car and an ambulance followed the fire truck as it turned into the farm lane. When Elias motioned, a cop and an EMT ran toward them.

Fifteen minutes later, the fire was doused. Smoke drifted from hot spots, but the firefighters drenched those areas with water. The front wall of the shop was charred, but the rest of the building had suffered only smoke and water damage. The goods inside would have to be cleaned, but they weren't destroyed.

Sarah Beth thanked every first responder, but the twins' idea of serving cookies brought broader smiles from them. She prepared Kaffi and ice tea and shared it with everyone as they gathered their equipment and stored it away so it'd be ready for the next emergency.

Sudden shouts shattered the joviality. She looked at where Mahlon was jabbing his chin at Elias. He couldn't use a finger, because he wore handcuffs.

"You can't blame us for our pranks without blaming him too," Mahlon yelled at the policeman who stood beside him, but the officer was talking on his radio, paying no attention to Mahlon's rants. He looked over at Vera, who was being treated for a bruised forehead. "She was furious because *he* used to slap her around. No man should be allowed to treat a woman like that. You should arrest *him* for abuse!"

Sarah Beth was ready to jump to Elias's defense again, but he answered before she could.

His voice was calm and filled with pity as he said, "I'm sorry she mixed you up in her schemes, Mahlon." He sighed as he held the other man's gaze until Mahlon looked away. "I've never raised my hand to her or any woman." Turning to Vera, he said, "You owe him the truth."

"I don't owe him anything," she spat. "If he'd done what he was supposed to, we'd have convinced you and the Kings to leave. You would have been penniless, which I would have enjoyed watching while I lived on this farm with my husband. Not you. You had your chance to marry me, Elias, but you blew it."

"All of this because I didn't walk out with you years ago?"

Mahlon cried, "You lied to me, Vera? I thought you loved me. I wouldn't have risked my horse and buggy to send my Daed's buggy into the ditch if I'd known you wanted Elias instead."

Sarah Beth wasn't the only one who gasped at Mahlon's admission that he'd been the one who could have killed two reckless young men racing their buggies. The policeman cautioned him not to say anything else before he had a lawyer. Putting Mahlon in the car, he repeated the warning to Vera as he drew her hands behind her and locked cuffs around them.

As Vera was put into the car, Elias whispered, "It's finally over."

17

Elias was wrong.

The next week, Martin Rodriguez returned to the Kings' farm. Sarah Beth sent Toby to bring Elias to the house.

"I wanted you to hear this right away," the deputy said while they waited for Elias to arrive. He smiled at the twins. "Are you visiting here again today?"

They shook their heads, but didn't speak.

"They're going to be living here," Sarah Beth explained.

Uriah had handled the reunion with his usual deftness, kindness, and tact. After a single conversation with their Aenti and Onkel, during which he reminded them how hard Sarah Beth was working to get the damaged shop ready to open so she could provide for her whole family, it was decided that the twins would return to Hickory Meadows but would spend one weekend each month in Ronks.

"I'm glad you've gotten your family together." He winked at the girls. "You're as cute as your big sisters."

The twins giggled but lowered their heads, abashed by the compliment from the tall Englischer.

When Elias walked in and joined them at the table, Cora put a cup of Kaffi in front of him and hurried to the counter where she could watch without having to say anything.

"What did you want us to hear right away?" Sarah Beth asked, too curious to wait any longer.

The deputy became businesslike again as he turned to Elias.

"I wanted you to hear what Vera Swartzentruber told us when we questioned her again."

"Is she all right?" he asked. "I know how terrifying an interrogation can be."

He arched his brows. "I've heard a lot about you Amish and how you forgive those who do bad things to you."

"Forgiveness is never easy." He unclasped his hands and put one over Sarah Beth's. "It's no easier for plain folk than for anyone else. However, if one wishes to be forgiven for his mistakes, one must learn to forgive those who have hurt him and those he loves."

"If more people felt the way you do, we'd have fewer revenge crimes to deal with." He picked up his cup and took an appreciative sip. "Vera said you and her brother Roy were good friends."

"We were. Once." He didn't explain further.

"Then I'm sorry to tell you that Vera has confirmed that her brother was the one who put your phone in the hay."

"He did?"

"He thought it would be funny if your phone was found and you got into trouble for having it. When the fire started by what we now believe was spontaneous combustion, he let you take the blame because he feared he'd be arrested too."

"At least he never confirmed it was my phone, so I had to be released."

"An odd sort of friend, if you ask me."

Sarah Beth agreed with the policeman, but she didn't say anything as she rose and brought two pieces of peach pie Cora was cutting to the table. She set one in front of each man.

"What will happen to them?" she asked.

"As far as Roy, he didn't do anything legally wrong. It's different for Mahlon and Vera. They have serious charges against them, including hit-and-run as well as arson. Once they're indicted, it's likely they'll make a plea bargain and have to serve only a short time in prison." He took a bite of the pie and grinned. "I've got to stop by more often. This is delicious, Sarah Beth."

"Stop anytime you're in the area. There will always be something sweet for you here."

"Unless we've eaten it," Cora added with her customary bluntness. Everyone laughed.

As Elias worked on Abe's buggy, he said prayers for comfort for the older man as well as Mahlon and Vera. He knew how frightened they must be.

He heard the door open. Was it Toby? He'd hired the boy back yesterday evening, but Toby had commitments to his other employers as well as the family farm, so Elias wasn't sure when he'd arrive.

When he saw Harry Fitzgerald walk in, Elias rose to his feet.

Without a greeting, Harry said, "I owe you an apology, Elias."

"I can't imagine why."

His landlord held up his hand. "Let me say what I've gotta say."

"Go ahead."

"I've had my eye on buying the empty storefront across the street from Yoder's for a few years. I'd asked Abe Yoder if he'd sell it to me. I was pretty sure I could rent it. Whether he was worried about the competition of another business or had plans of his own, he'd never say. A few months ago, after you moved in here, Yoder's son stopped by my place and suggested that if I got you to leave, he'd work on his father to sell me the empty store. I resisted at first, but he said the deal would go through if I convinced you to move. He never told me why he wanted you to leave." He hung his head. "I'm ashamed that I let my greed to get the property play me into Mahlon's hands. You've been a good tenant, and I should have told him to get lost."

"Did he suggest I move to your other property?"

"No. He just wanted you gone from Hickory Meadows."

Elias put his hand on his landlord's shoulder. "There's no need for shame. I can't say what I would have done if our situations were reversed, but I hope I would have been as generous as you were toward me when you offered me the other place."

"I acted like his puppet." He glanced back as the door opened and Sarah Beth walked in. With a broad smile, Harry went on, "You're welcome to stay here as long as you'd like." He held out his hand.

Elias shook it. "Danki, Harry."

Sarah Beth said nothing until Harry had gotten into his car. Setting the basket she'd brought onto Elias's worktable, she drew the cloth off the top.

"I thought you might like another piece of the peach pie." As she lifted it out, she asked, "Was Harry still trying to talk you into moving?"

"The opposite."

When he explained, she was shocked. She hadn't guessed Mahlon's scheme was so far-reaching.

"I'm happy for you, Elias. You've worked hard, and you've turned your cheek to those who would hurt you. You deserve to have everything you've wanted."

"I don't have everything." He gave her a crooked smile. "I'm not sure I want to stay here."

Her chest hurt as if someone had seized her heart and crushed it. Putting her hand over it, she whispered, "You don't?"

What a fool she'd been! Right from the day Elias had told her he might be moving his business, she'd known it would be stupid to let him become a part of her life and her family's lives. Why hadn't she listened to herself?

Instead she'd followed her heart to him. She'd fought it every step of the way, but that hadn't made any difference. She'd fallen in love with him.

"I'm not planning to leave Hickory Meadows." He cupped her chin and tilted her face so his gaze caught hers. "That is . . . if you'll be willing to let me use an outbuilding on your farm for my shop after we're married."

"Married?" she whispered. "You want to marry me?"

"Why not?" He gave her a mischievous grin. "I'm already beginning to feel like part of your family."

"You *are* a part of our family." A smile erupted across her face as she said the words she'd held inside her heart for what seemed now like her whole life, waiting for the right man to speak them to. "I love you, Elias Stutzman, and ja, I want to marry you if you'll have me."

"You know I love you too, ain't so?"

"Ja." She'd seen the truth in his eyes and felt it within her heart. When he pulled her into his arms, he kissed her with the love he had to share with her for the rest of their lives, and this time he was in no hurry.

Learn more about Annie's fiction books at

AnniesFiction.com

- Access your e-books
- Discover exciting new series
- Read sample chapters
- Watch video book trailers
- Share your feedback

We've designed the Annie's Fiction website especially for you!

Plus, manage your account online!

- Check your account status
- Make payments online
- Update your address

Visit us at AnniesFiction.com